DEATH AT AURORA POINT

A TILLY LAFLEUR MYSTERY
BOOK 2

MAISIE GRAVES

TWISTED DAFFODIL PUBLISHING

LANGUAGE NOTE

This book was written in Canada, by a Canadian, about Canadians—so yes, the spelling is a little different. We do things like add "u" where others wouldn't, use "fibre" instead of "fiber," and don't blink twice at a "cheque."

Canadian English is a glorious mix of American, British, French-Canadian, and Indigenous influences. It's quirky, it's correct—and it's completely intentional.

So if something looks odd, just blame the maple syrup and carry on. We've got mysteries to solve.

- Maisie

S team curled from sturdy mugs of coffee, folding chairs creaked against the floor, and the northern lights waited on the horizon—ready to put Balsam Bay on the map, whether we liked it or not.

I sat at the long table in the community centre on Friday morning, Des curled at my feet like she was the only one here not bracing for battle. Which, considering the committee members assembled, wasn't far off. Mabel Whitfield had commandeered the head of the table, flanked by a clipboard, a water bottle, and enough sticky notes to wallpaper the moon. The former town librarian—and the unofficial keeper of every story Balsam Bay ever told—had been steering the event since the astronomy club first dreamed it up five years ago, equal parts civic cheerleader and logistics wrangler.

What started as informal stargazing gatherings at Aurora Point had exploded into something none of us had planned for. Between Callie's blog coverage and the unfortunate media attention our town had received from the summer's events, we were looking at six to seven hundred visitors in a community of just under four thousand. The hundred-campsite facility was already at capacity, the Lantern Inn was booked solid, and cabin rentals were up.

"I'm just saying," Mabel announced, stabbing a pen toward the paper in front of her, "if we don't finalize the vendor layout today, I'll be forced to make the executive decision to put the donut hole stand beside the axe-throwing booth again—and we all remember how that went."

"That guy signed the release form," someone mumbled from the back.

"You still owe me a first aid kit," added Kelli Bough from across the table. She ran the little wellness shop near the museum and had become a surprisingly steady presence in town, despite arriving barely a year ago with two Himalayan salt lamps and no winter boots.

Next to me, Callie clicked away on her tablet, managing volunteer signups while simultaneously documenting everything for her blog. She'd been quietly turning the festival into a social media darling for weeks now, and the results showed—hashtags like #BalsamBayBlazesBright and #AuroraNightsVibes were trending in tourism circles. My daughter had a knack for spotting opportunity, especially when it involved a camera or a cause.

"I do want to flag something," said a new voice, quieter, with the careful tone of someone who expected to be ignored. Arlo Trent—science teacher, amateur astronomer, and Balsam Bay's official northern lights forecaster—adjusted his glasses. "Solar activity is unusually high right now. The auroras might be visible for most of the week, not just the peak nights. That's going to bring in a lot more people than usual."

"That's the idea," Callie said brightly, never looking up from her tablet.

"Yes, but—" Arlo hesitated. "There's a difference between a

nice crowd and a... surge. I've already had three calls from out-of-province tour operators asking if we offer shuttle access to Aurora Point."

The room stilled.

Bertha Wise, who'd kept the general store running with more efficiency than some government offices, cleared her throat. "And what did you tell them?"

"That it's protected Crown land, and the last thing we need is busloads of people stomping all over it," Arlo said. "Which is true. But I think we should be prepared. The trail access is challenging enough without dealing with crowds who don't know the terrain."

A sharp click interrupted him. Charlotte Bugle—seated near the end of the table like a potted plant with a spreadsheet—had finally decided to weigh in.

"Well," she said with a smile sharp enough to cut glass, "the mayor's office has actually anticipated the possibility of increased interest in Aurora Point."

The mayor's office. As if they'd been involved from the beginning instead of swooping in at the last minute with premium packages and media coordination. And of course Charlotte—Mayor John Bugle's niece—was here now, the first Bugle ever to sit on the festival committee. Mabel might hold the title of committee head, but Charlotte had been introducing herself as festival coordinator since the day she arrived, and no one had found the nerve to correct her.

"Which is why," Charlotte continued smoothly, "I've invited Dawn Kessler to document the festival. She's a travel and science blogger with a podcast that reaches thousands of people interested in natural phenomena, and she's developed quite a following with her travel segments documenting unique Canadian destinations. She'll be capturing the authentic community experience."

"Dawn Kessler?" Fern Carrick—our resident astronomy enthusiast and museum staffer, normally the last person to raise her voice in a crowd—called from the coffee urn, mug suspended mid-pour. "*The* Dawn Kessler from Canadian Cosmic Conversations?" Her face lit up with genuine excitement. "I can't believe you didn't tell us! I've been following her work for years—she did that incredible series on light pollution and its impact on wildlife migration patterns."

Across the table, I noticed Arlo's pen freeze mid-note, his eyes widening for just a moment before he looked down at his papers with sudden, intense focus.

"Dawn specializes in making science accessible," Charlotte explained. "Her work bridges the gap between academic research and public understanding. Exactly what we need to position Balsam Bay as a serious aurora destination."

"I'm particularly interested in how communities balance preservation with tourism," said a new voice from the back of the room. Dawn Kessler herself had quietly slipped into the room, notebook in hand, observing with the careful attention of someone already working. "Especially when there are... competing interests about land use. Economic development versus environmental protection. Old families versus newcomers. Those tensions make for compelling storytelling."

At Dawn's sudden appearance, Fern's coffee mug tilted dangerously, sending a small cascade over the rim that she hastily dabbed with a napkin, her cheeks flushing with what looked like a combination of excitement and nerves.

The woman was maybe in her late thirties, with the kind of confident bearing that came from asking difficult questions for a living. She'd already found her way to the back corner where she could observe without disrupting—professional instincts, probably.

"Welcome, Dawn," Charlotte said, undoubtedly enjoying

Dawn's timing. "Dawn's brought her travel trailer," Charlotte added. "She'll be staying at the festival campground for the full experience—really immersing herself in the community story."

"Why don't I get perspectives from multiple people?" Dawn suggested diplomatically. "The more voices, the richer the story."

"Perfect," Callie said, finally looking up from her tablet. "I've been documenting a lot of the festival prep on my blog. Happy to share insights from the social media angle."

And just like that, my daughter had inserted herself into whatever media circus was brewing. It wasn't surprising—Callie had inherited my curiosity along with my stubborn streak.

"Wonderful," Dawn said, making a note. "This is exactly the kind of authentic community engagement I was hoping to find."

Authentic. The word was starting to lose all meaning.

Across the table, Charlie Campbell sat quietly beside Charlotte, the picture of devoted attention. Museum volunteer, occasional handyman, and, according to local gossip, Charlotte's boyfriend. Sean Patrick—Balsam Bay's unofficial geologist-in-residence—had mentioned that Charlie had been spending time at the museum this week, apparently eager to help with everything from display arrangements to cataloguing mineral samples.

"I could help coordinate anything you need," Charlie offered suddenly, addressing Dawn directly. "Museum access, transportation around town, whatever would be useful."

I caught the brief, restraining touch of Charlotte's hand on his arm—a gesture that looked affectionate but carried the unmistakable weight of a leash. "That's sweet of you, but I'm sure Dawn and her team have everything under control."

Charlie's eager expression dimmed slightly, but he nodded. "Of course. Just wanted to offer."

The dismissal was so smooth he probably didn't even realize it had happened. But I caught the flicker of disappointment in his eyes before he covered it with another obliging smile.

"Right then," Mabel said, clearly wanting to regain control of her meeting. "Should we get back to vendor layouts? We still need to finalize the food court setup and coordinate with the fire marshal about the lantern walks."

"Of course," Dawn said, settling back with her notebook. "Don't mind me. I'm just observing."

Sure she was. And Des was just a dog who happened to be uncannily good at reading people.

The meeting lurched back into logistics mode—vendor permits, volunteer schedules, the eternal question of portable toilets versus the community centre washrooms. Someone mentioned coordinating with LANTERN for campground management, which earned a few eye rolls from people scattered around the room.

"Sorry," Dawn piped up from her observer's perch, pen hovering over her notebook. "What's LANTERN?"

"Local Alliance for Nature, Tourism, and Environmental Resilience," Fern explained brightly. "They're focused on conservation and making sure the festival stays sustainable."

"And CLAIM is the opposite," Arlo muttered. "Citizens for Local Access, Industry, and Mining. They want development back—especially the mine."

CLAIM supporters weren't fond of LANTERN's environmental restrictions, especially when they slowed down practical festival logistics. Even during festival planning, the town's competing land-use groups couldn't seem to avoid their disagreements.

But I kept catching glimpses of Dawn making notes during seemingly mundane discussions. What was worth documenting about the debate over whether to use battery-powered or solar string lights?

And why did Charlotte look like she'd won something every time Dawn wrote something down?

Sean caught my eye from across the room, that familiar half-smile playing at the corners of his mouth. He'd been around long enough to blur the line between visitor and neighbour. Officially, he was writing a book about Balsam Bay's geology. Unofficially, his private contract work in the area kept a small distance between us that neither of us quite knew how to cross.

"Can you give us some specifics on the aurora forecast, Arlo?" Sean asked.

Arlo brightened immediately. "Exceptional conditions this week. The geomagnetic storm that's building should give us displays visible even through town lighting. Aurora Point itself..." He paused, glancing around the table. "Well, it's going to be magical. That elevated amphitheatre effect makes the lights seem like they're dancing just for you."

"Life-changing moments," Fern added softly, her voice carrying the reverence of someone who'd spent years sharing that experience with visitors. "That's what people remember. That's what brings them back."

"Which is exactly what we want," Charlotte said. "Sustainable tourism built around our natural advantages."

The Bugles had always been more interested in resource development opportunities—reopening the mine, expanding commercial ventures—than following the tourism-focused direction that Balsam Bay founder Sam Melvin had established decades ago. It aligned them perfectly with CLAIM's development agenda. But her tone suggested something different—

tourism that could be managed, controlled, monetized. The kind that came with infrastructure and development and all the things that made places like Aurora Point less magical and more profitable.

Dawn looked up from her notes. "How does the community handle access to Aurora Point? It sounds like there are capacity concerns."

"We've worked out a rotation system," Bertha explained. "Everyone gets one special Aurora Point experience during their visit. Managed access to Crown land with minimal environmental impact. Everyone takes turns, everyone respects the space."

"Though this year the mayor's office has approved a 'premium viewing experience' for select guests," Charlotte added smoothly. "Limited numbers, for those who want a more... curated experience."

There was a beat of stunned silence. Curated. Like the magic of Aurora Point needed editing.

"You added a what?" Kelli asked.

"Exclusive guided transportation, light refreshments, private viewing area. It's all being handled professionally."

I sat forward. "And how exactly are you planning to keep the 'exclusive' guests from trampling all over an unsupervised stretch of protected land with documented erosion issues?"

Charlotte's smile didn't falter. "The same way we do everything else, Ms. Lafleur—with the town's best interests at heart."

I didn't trust anyone who used that phrase. Especially not someone with the last name Bugle.

"Is this really what the festival is about now?" I asked. "Private upgrades and tourist targeting? Or are we still pretending this is a community event?"

Charlotte's expression cooled by a few degrees. "Your concerns are noted."

Which, in Bugle-speak, meant "watch your step."

Callie paused her typing. Bertha raised an eyebrow at me. Des gave a sigh that sounded suspiciously like, "you poked the bear again, didn't you?"

"Interesting," Dawn said, writing furiously. "Balancing preservation with access—that's always a fascinating challenge."

By the time we wrapped up—vendor layouts finalized, Des officially dubbed "festival mascot" after Callie's enthusiastic lobbying, and promises to reconvene tomorrow—I had more questions than answers.

"That was productive," Callie said as we gathered our things. "I like Dawn. She seems really interested in getting the story right."

"Mm," I said, watching as Charlotte approached Dawn near the door, already deep in conversation about interview schedules and "key messaging opportunities."

Des stretched and padded toward the exit, pausing to sniff at Dawn's boots as she passed. Dawn bent down automatically to give her a quick pat, the gesture natural and unthinking.

"Friendly dog," Dawn said, smiling up at me.

"She's got good instincts about people," I replied, studying Dawn's face for any flicker of reaction.

If there was one, I missed it. Dawn just smiled and returned to her conversation with Charlotte.

Outside, the autumn sun was warming the streets, casting everything in that golden light that made even mundane committee meetings feel like the beginning of something important. The festival banners strung across Main Street fluttered in the breeze, and volunteers in matching t-shirts were already setting up the information booth.

But as we walked toward the car, I found myself thinking about the morning's dynamics. Something felt off-balance, though I couldn't quite put my finger on what. Maybe it was just the way Charlotte had positioned herself as Dawn's primary contact, or how smoothly she'd managed every interaction.

Or maybe it was simpler than that—just the unsettled feeling that came with watching your hometown get repackaged for outside consumption, even with the best of intentions.

The festival was happening. The question was: whose version of Balsam Bay would end up in Dawn's podcast?

Outside the community centre, the committee members scattered to their various afternoon plans. Fern was already deep in conversation with Arlo about scouting locations for the telescope setup, their voices animated with excitement about the week's forecast. Sean caught my eye and nodded toward his truck with a questioning look—probably wondering if I wanted to grab coffee and catch up.

"Rain check?" I called to him. "Callie and I are grabbing lunch."

He smiled and waved, heading off toward the museum.

"Actually, speaking of lunch," Callie said, pulling out her phone to check something, "I should respond to a few comments on the blog post first. People are already asking about festival parking and whether pets are allowed at events." She leaned against the car, fingers flying over the screen. "This'll just take a few minutes."

I watched the last of the committee members drive away

while Callie worked. Charlie had lingered near the community centre steps, apparently waiting for Charlotte, but she'd walked straight past him toward Main Street without a backward glance. He'd stood there for a moment, looking uncertain, before finally heading to his own truck.

"Okay, done," Callie said, tucking her phone away. "Want to grab lunch at The Lumberjack's Daughter? I could go for one of Mandy's grilled cheese and tomato soup combos."

"Sounds good," I said, but my attention was already drifting toward the warm glow spilling from the café windows across the street. Through the glass, I could see the familiar lunch crowd settling in for coffee and conversation.

"Let me just grab my charger," Callie said, opening the car door. "Phone's dying, and I want to post about Des's official mascot status while people are still talking about the meeting."

Des trotted alongside me as we crossed toward the café, her tags jingling softly in the crisp air. Early October had that perfect edge promising cooler temperatures—ideal aurora weather, according to Arlo's forecasts.

I was adjusting my jacket against the autumn chill when movement through the café's front windows caught my eye. Three figures at the corner table, heads bent together in conversation. Charlotte sat with her back to the street, perfectly composed even in casual discussion. Across from her, Dawn leaned forward with her notebook open, nodding at whatever Charlotte was explaining. And beside Charlotte sat a third figure—Mayor John Bugle himself, looking more engaged than I'd seen him in weeks.

The full Bugle operation, apparently.

"Mom?" Callie appeared at my elbow, charger cable in hand. "You coming in?"

"In a minute," I said, still watching the scene unfold. My SAR training had taught me to observe before acting, to read the landscape before making assumptions. Right now, the social landscape inside that café was telling me a story I wasn't sure I liked. "Just trying to figure something out."

Through the window, John was talking now, gesturing with the kind of animated enthusiasm he usually reserved for town council meetings when discussing economic development. Dawn smiled politely, but her attention clearly remained focused on Charlotte. Charlotte, for her part, managed the conversation with the smooth efficiency of someone accustomed to controlling information flow.

As we pushed through the door, the bell announcing our arrival, I caught the tail end of their discussion.

"—really important for people to understand the broader context," John was saying. "This festival represents more than just tourism. It's about positioning Balsam Bay as a destination with real economic potential."

"Absolutely," Dawn agreed, making notes. "The intersection of community identity and development pressures is fascinating. How do you balance growth with preservation?"

"Carefully," Charlotte said with a practiced smile. "That's why bringing in the right voices is so important. People who understand the vision."

The vision. Not the community's vision, apparently, but something more selective. Something curated.

The café door chimed, and Charlie entered, scanning the room until he spotted Charlotte's table. He approached with the hopeful expression of someone who wasn't sure if he'd be welcome, but was willing to try anyway.

"Mind if I join you?" Charlie asked quietly, already pulling out the chair beside Charlotte.

"We were just discussing the media coverage angle," Charlotte said, patting his hand briefly. "Nothing you haven't heard before."

Charlie nodded, settling into his seat with the careful movements of someone trying not to disrupt the flow of conversation. He listened intently as John continued explaining the town's development vision, occasionally glancing at Charlotte as if seeking approval for his presence.

"That's fascinating," Dawn said, making notes. "The balance between preserving character and encouraging growth—it's a challenge every small community faces."

Charlie brightened, clearly seeing an opening. "The museum displays really show that evolution. We've got mining artifacts right next to astronomy equipment, old logging tools beside recently-collected geological samples. It's like the whole town's story in one building."

Charlotte's smile tightened almost imperceptibly. "Charlie's been very... enthusiastic about the museum work."

The subtle emphasis on 'enthusiastic' carried just enough condescension to sting, though Charlie's eager expression suggested he'd missed the barb entirely.

"Tilly!" Dawn looked up as we approached their table, her face brightening with genuine warmth. "Perfect timing. I was just telling Charlotte and John how much I'm looking forward to exploring everything Balsam Bay has to offer."

"It's a special place," I said carefully, nodding to the assembled Bugles and Charlie. "I hope you get to see all sides of it."

"That's exactly what I'm hoping for," Dawn said. "The more perspectives I can gather, the richer the story becomes. Charlotte mentioned you used to be involved in search and rescue? That must give you a unique view of the landscape."

"Among other things," I said, aware of Charlotte and the

mayor's sharp attention. "There's a lot of territory to cover around here. Different people know different pieces of it."

"I'd love to talk to anyone willing to share their perspective," Dawn continued. "Local historians, business owners, longtime residents. The whole spectrum."

John leaned forward. "Well, you're talking to the right people for that. The Bugle family's been here for generations. We've seen this town through a lot of changes."

"That's wonderful," Dawn said, making another note. "Generational perspective is so valuable. But I'm also interested in newer voices—people who've chosen to make Balsam Bay home more recently. How that changes the community dynamic."

Charlotte's smile tightened almost imperceptibly. "Of course. Though it's important to separate those who are truly invested in Balsam Bay's future from those who still keep one foot elsewhere. If you're not fully committed, it shows."

A pointed comment—everyone knew I still had a condo in Victoria. The remark landed like a quiet warning, and Charlie shifted uncomfortably beside her.

"Speaking of community," John said, turning his attention to me, "Tilly, I wanted to mention—tomorrow's memorial service for your father—just wanted to confirm everything's still on schedule. The whole town's looking forward to paying their respects." His tone carried the satisfied weight of someone who'd finally gotten his way after months of gentle pressure.

The way he said it—like it was his event to coordinate—made my teeth itch. "Yes, everything's arranged."

It was true, though tomorrow's service weighed on me more heavily than I cared to admit. Between Charlotte's maneuvering and Dawn's eager questions, my mind kept circling back to what it would feel like to stand at the lakeshore with the whole town watching, pretending to say goodbye.

Dawn looked between us with the careful expression of someone who'd just realized they'd walked into something personal. "I should probably focus on the festival coverage," she said diplomatically. "I'd love to talk to anyone willing to share their perspective about the community's relationship with the landscape."

"Actually," I found myself saying, "you should definitely talk to Sean Patrick. He's a geologist who's been doing interesting work in the area. Really understands the landscape that makes Balsam Bay so special."

"Sean's work is rather... technical," Charlotte said quickly. "I'm not sure it would translate well for a general audience."

"Actually, that sounds perfect," Dawn said, making a note despite Charlotte's obvious displeasure. "I love incorporating scientific context. Helps listeners understand why these places are genuinely special, not just pretty."

"Sean would eat that up," Charlie said suddenly, his face lighting up with the chance to contribute something useful. "Guy's been teaching me about mineral compositions at the museum. Really knows his stuff about the local geology."

Charlotte looked less than thrilled by this development, but covered it smoothly. "Well, if you think it would add value to the story..."

"Definitely. Tilly, do you know how I could reach Sean?"

"He mentioned he was planning to spend the afternoon at the museum working on some festival displays," I said. "Fern could introduce you."

Which would give Fern more time with Dawn—something that clearly didn't sit well with Charlotte judging by the way her fingers drummed against the table.

"Perfect," Dawn said. "This is exactly the kind of authentic detail that makes a story come alive."

There was that word again—authentic—polished smooth by overuse. And it wasn't Dawn I was worried about so much as Charlotte... her version of authentic versus what the rest of us might consider genuine community spirit. I'd spent enough time around media attention to know the difference between authentic and "authentic," packaged and presented for easy consumption.

From the look on Charlotte's face, I was pretty sure I knew which version we were dealing with.

"Well," Charlotte said, gathering her purse with decisive efficiency, "we should let you enjoy your lunch, Tilly. Dawn, shall we continue our discussion at the hotel later since you said you'd be getting your crew settled in there? I can arrange for you to speak with some key community figures."

Key community figures. Translation: people Charlotte could control.

"Sounds great," Dawn said, closing her notebook. "And Charlie, thanks for the geology tip. I might take you up on that museum tour."

Charlie practically glowed at the acknowledgment.

As they filed out together, John and Charlotte flanking Dawn like an honour guard while Charlie trailed slightly behind, I found myself thinking about access and control. Aurora Point was Crown land—public space that couldn't be owned or sold. But that didn't mean it couldn't be managed, marketed, and packaged for the right kind of visitor.

The question was: what kind of visitors did the Bugles want? And what were they willing to do to ensure they got them?

"Interesting dynamics," Callie murmured, sliding into the seat Charlotte had vacated.

"Very," I agreed, still thinking about the way Charlotte had orchestrated that entire interaction. Dawn might think she was conducting interviews, but Charlotte was clearly managing the narrative.

Mandy appeared at our table with her usual warm smile. "Afternoon, ladies. I heard you had quite the committee meeting."

Callie laughed. "At least Des finally got her moment in the spotlight."

"About time that dog got proper recognition," Mandy said, bending to give Des a scratch behind the ears. "She's been the unofficial town ambassador for months. Half the tourists who come through here ask about her after seeing Callie's blog posts."

"She does love the attention," I said, giving Des a pat. "And it's nice to see the town in such good spirits, especially with the festival ramping up."

Mandy nodded, glancing toward the window where volunteers bustled past. "That's the best part of this time of year—everyone pitches in. Reminds you why small towns work. Now, what can I get you two for lunch?"

As Mandy headed to the kitchen, I found myself studying the scene outside the window. Festival volunteers continued their setup work, tourists wandered with cameras and coffee cups—everything looked perfectly normal for a town preparing to welcome hundreds of visitors.

But normal had a way of hiding complicated truths. I'd learned that lesson thoroughly this summer, when Dad's disappearance had revealed layers of community secrets I'd never suspected.

The difference this time was that I wasn't starting from scratch. This time, I knew to look for the currents underneath the surface—and I was pretty sure Charlotte Bugle was counting on no one bothering to look that deep.

Des stretched under the table and looked up at me with those knowing brown eyes, as if she could sense the direction of my thoughts.

"Don't worry, girl," I murmured, scratching behind her ears. "Just keeping watch."

After all, someone had to.

CHAPTER TWO

The morning of Dad's memorial service arrived grey and still, the kind of day that felt like the world was holding its breath. I'd barely slept, my mind cycling between festival logistics and the impossible weight of pretending to grieve someone who wasn't dead. Now, with two hours until the church service, our kitchen had become command central for the final arrangements.

My brother Jason sat at the table nursing his second cup of coffee, already in his RCMP dress uniform out of respect for Dad. The formality of it looked strange in our familiar kitchen, but it felt right for today. Callie moved between the counter and the stove, making sandwiches we probably wouldn't eat but that gave her something to do with her hands.

Bertha stood in the living room over the memorial box Joe Charles, Dad's closest friend and a seasoned dog musher from the outskirts of town, had made. Her hands moving with practiced efficiency. Joe had carved it from planks salvaged from the old canoe he and Walter once fished from—the grain still holding the faint scent of lake water and forty years of summer mornings. Inside, she'd arranged Dad's reading glasses, folded on top of his favourite flannel shirt, and a faded photo of him and Jason grinning over a northern pike. In one corner rested a small coin box—what had begun as Walter's casual hobby had grown into a collection worth several thousand dollars, the kind of legacy the museum would prize.

"Found these in his desk," she added, tucking a thick manila envelope and a smaller cream-coloured one alongside the keepsakes. "Old photos and papers—seemed right to keep them together."

I turned away from the box, my chest tightening. "Whatever you think is right."

Bertha glanced up, her expression soft with concern. "Tilly, maybe you should—"

"No." The word came out sharper than I intended. Two hours until the memorial; by the end of today everything would be packed away in the museum, Walter officially part of Balsam Bay's history. Bertha believed she was helping us say goodbye, but I couldn't pretend to grieve someone who was still alive.

Des whined from her spot by the door, the soft anxious sound she made when too many things changed at once.

"I know, girl." I scratched behind her ears. "Almost over."

Bertha lifted a small wooden carving from Dad's desk—a loon he'd whittled the summer after my mother died. Her thumb traced its smooth surface before placing it carefully beside the photos. "Said keeping his hands busy helped with the quiet."

My throat tightened. I needed air, movement, anything but standing here watching Dad's life get arranged for display.

Callie appeared in the doorway, car keys jingling in her hand. "Jason's ready. We should head to the church early, get everything positioned."

Bertha closed the box with deliberate care, running her hands along Joe's precise joints like she was sealing something sacred. "Your father would be proud. Both of you, handling this with such grace."

Grace. If that's what they wanted to call the numbness that let me function, fine.

I reached for my jacket. "Ready?"

The drive to Balsam Bay United Church passed in silence —Des's head resting against my shoulder in the back seat. Jason followed in his cruiser, the memorial box secured beside him.

The church smelled like lemon oil and decades of Sunday mornings as we carried the box inside. Walter's memorial had drawn the entire community, their voices rising in familiar hymns that would have made him smile.

The hardest part wasn't grief—it was pretending. Every testimony, every tear, every gentle touch on my shoulder pressed down like a weight. Dad was safe, hidden away after the Bugles' threats had made staying in Balsam Bay impossible. His canoeing accident was the cover story—his death, a necessary lie that only Jason, Callie, and I carried.

But the grief in this room was real. We weren't mourning Walter. We were mourning our ability to tell the truth.

Beside me, Callie sat quietly in her dark sweater, chosen for today's performance. Jason occupied the seat on my other side, his uniform crisp and formal, his presence both supportive and appropriately official. Des pressed against my leg, her warm weight a steady reminder that some loyalties transcended understanding.

The pews were packed with neighbours, shopkeepers, old fishing buddies, and summer residents. We'd slipped into the third row—close enough to see everyone, far enough that no one would study our faces too closely. I couldn't bear the front row, not when the man we were supposed to be mourning wasn't gone at all.

I saw Charlotte near the front, her head bowed in what looked like genuine respect. Beside her sat the mayor, his expression arranged into solemnity, though the corners of his mouth twitched like a man privately pleased with how the day was unfolding. Whatever else I thought about Charlotte's political manoeuvring, she'd known Walter her whole life. Her grief, at least, seemed real. John's—I wasn't so sure.

Near the back, Sean caught my eye and offered a small nod. His presence felt like quiet solidarity—someone who understood grief could be complicated.

The Balsam Belles had claimed an entire pew, their usual chatter replaced by solemn attention. Enid, Nora, and Trish—Walter's self-appointed fan club and the town's unofficial news network—looked uncharacteristically subdued today. Bertha, at the very front, sat straight-backed, hands steady on a worn prayer book. If anyone here had the right to mourn Walter, it was her.

At the pulpit, Reverend Nichols spoke of Walter's quiet generosity, his decades of service, the way he'd made everyone who walked into his store feel welcome. The stories were real, and that made this whole charade harder to bear.

"Walter never sought recognition," he said. "But if you needed groceries when money was tight, or a ride when your car broke down, or just someone to listen, he was there."

Murmurs of agreement rippled through the congregation.

When memories were invited, the stories came in a steady stream. Walter teaching kids to tie fishing knots. Driving Mrs. Peterson to appointments. Staying late to help hunters load supplies. Each small kindness built a portrait of a man who'd shaped this town in ways both big and small.

Joe sat quietly until a pause opened. Then he rose, not to

speak, but to nod once toward the memorial display. A brief, wordless gesture that somehow carried more weight than speeches.

"He never made you feel stupid for not knowing something," Kelli offered. "Even when I first moved here and didn't know the difference between a life jacket and a PFD, he just explained it like it was the most natural question in the world."

More nods. More murmurs of recognition.

Jason stood, cleared his throat, and simply said: "He was the best man I've ever known. And I miss him." Then he sat.

The simplicity hit harder than anything else. Around me, people were nodding, crying, holding each other. The truth of Walter's impact was written in every face, but beneath my own grief sat the hollow knowledge that this celebration was happening without him.

As the service drew to a close, Reverend Nichols spoke of the evening's lakeside ceremony. "We'll gather at sunset to release lanterns in Walter's memory. The memorial display will be there as well, so those who'd like can spend a moment with his personal effects before they're housed at the museum."

At the front, John maintained his carefully solemn pose, while Charlotte shifted in her seat, pulling out her phone. She checked the screen quickly, fingers drumming against her designer purse before tucking it away.

Jason rose to collect the memorial box.

"Beautiful service," Callie said quietly. "Grandpa would have appreciated how simple it was."

"He would have," Jason replied, lifting it carefully.

People moved slowly, reluctant to leave, as if lingering could extend their connection to Walter's memory. Jason caught my eye, the box under his arm, his expression unreadable but supportive. He understood the burden we carried—

the impossible weight of keeping Walter's secret while watching genuine grief unfold.

As we stepped into the aisle, Callie leaned close. "The lakeside ceremony will feel different. He would have loved having it by the water."

She was right. Dad had always preferred the outdoors to formal spaces, the rhythms of the lake to the comfort of four walls. Tonight, under the open sky, we'd try again to say goodbye.

The lake was still when we arrived, its surface like dark glass reflecting the first hints of evening. Jason placed Dad's memorial box on a small table near the dock, the wood gleaming under the string lights Fern and her helpers had hung that morning. Rows of paper lanterns, handmade by community members over the past week, waited on wooden racks.

I stood near the back with Callie and Des, watching families find seats and friends gather in quiet clusters. The church service had been formal, contained within familiar walls. This, though, felt different—open to the night, threaded with the scent of pine and woodsmoke, as if the air itself wanted to hold us close.

"It feels like him," Callie murmured, her eyes on the lanterns.

The gentle informality of the lakeside setting, the way people moved freely between groups, sharing quiet stories—it felt more like Dad than any sermon ever could.

Overhead, a faint green shimmer began to dance across the northern horizon. Someone pointed, whispered. Heads tilted skyward.

Across the crowd, Fern lifted her gaze. "Aurora's starting

early tonight," she whispered, wonder softening her voice. The light brushed her cheek green as she glanced at Arlo, and for a breath their shared look seemed to hold something private.

Then she moved on, her pink toque bright against the darker coats and hoods as she and her volunteers threaded through the crowd, distributing lanterns with quiet hands. The Balsam Belles navigated the crowd with practiced grace—Nora pressing tissues into palms, Enid warning about the loose board at the dock's edge.

One lantern caught my eye—a cricket bat painted in pale blue, its neat lines worn around the edges. Sean's work. His embarrassing reality-show moment turned into a quiet tribute. I scanned the gathering but saw only familiar faces: Bertha, Charlotte, and Charlie standing slightly apart.

I chose a plain lantern. Callie picked one pressed with flowers. Together we knelt at the water's edge, coaxing the flames to life with fingers that trembled more than expected.

The duplicity made my stomach turn. We were sending lanterns for a man who wasn't gone, mourning a loss that wasn't real, while the people around us grieved with unguarded hearts.

One by one, lanterns drifted outward on the lake, bobbing like unmoored stars. Their light rippled against the water, a constellation loosened from the sky. Above, the aurora brightened—green ribbons folding over themselves, shimmering in silence. A child pointed upward, voice hushed with awe.

The moment felt fragile. Sacred. Like a spell we might break if we breathed too loudly.

Then came the low whir of a camera gimbal.

At first, I thought it might be Callie. But when I turned, I saw the tripod. The boom mic. The soft halo light.

And Dawn.

She stood at the edge of the gathering, her fresh gear too sharp for the night, her voice cutting through like glass.

"We're here at beautiful Balsam Bay, where the northern lights festival is just getting underway—"

Heads turned. Bertha froze mid-step.

"—and tonight's lakeside lantern ceremony is just one of the many ways this charming Manitoba town celebrates the magic of the auroras. As you can see behind me—"

"Oh my god," Callie whispered. "She thinks this is part of the festival."

Jason moved beside me, his face set like stone.

The silence now wasn't reverent. It was the silence of something broken.

"Excuse me," Fern called out, rising to her feet. "This is a private ceremony."

Dawn turned, confusion slipping into her smile. "I was told this was a public aurora event. Part of the festival programming."

"This is Walter McKay's memorial," Bertha said clearly. "A private remembrance for family and friends."

Dawn's composure faltered. "But I thought the memorial was at the church earlier. Someone from the committee told me this was part of Aurora Nights. They said filming the lantern release would make the perfect opening sequence." She gestured helplessly toward her crew. "We've been gathering material all day—this was supposed to be the highlight."

A ripple of disbelief moved through the crowd. Someone had lied to Dawn.

"There's been a misunderstanding," Charlotte said smoothly, stepping forward. "This is a private ceremony. We'll arrange alternative filming tomorrow."

Dawn's face had gone pale. "I'm so sorry. I had no idea. I

was given specific details about time and place. I thought this was official programming."

Her crew began to pack up, reading the room. Professionals knew the line between public spectacle and private grief.

The boom mic operator, a young man with an apologetic look, stepped backward—his heel catching on the very board Enid had warned about.

A muffled crack.

He stumbled. Arms flailed. The mic swung wide and he toppled into the rack of unlit lanterns.

A lantern hit flame. Tissue paper flared. Orange snapped through the dark.

Heat surged. Smoke curled upward, bitter and fast.

For a breath, no one moved. Then Kelli screamed. Callie clutched my arm.

Jason's jacket came off in a single motion. He slammed it over the flames, stamping hard. Wood hissed. Fabric scorched. The air filled with the acrid sting of smoke and burnt cloth.

The fire was out in seconds. But the magic was gone.

Lanterns lay scattered, some crushed, others drifting crooked in the water. Children sobbed, their tears rising sharp against the night. The smell of char lingered, turning the air harsh where it had been tender.

The sacred hush had collapsed into confusion, anger, intrusion.

People rose, voices sharp. Some headed for cars. Others clustered in tight knots.

"Who would do this?" Bertha's voice shook.

Someone had set Dawn up, used her as the blunt edge of disruption.

I scanned the faces—Charlotte's polished concern, Charlie's awkward shock, John Bugle's solemn mask stretched too tight over something almost pleased.

Dawn looked stricken, her distress too raw to be an act. Whatever her faults, she hadn't known. She'd been used.

Above us, the aurora kept its silent dance, ribbons rippling as though the sky didn't care.

As the crowd thinned, disappointment heavy in the air, my unease hardened into resolve. Whoever had done this hadn't just ruined a ceremony. They'd violated something sacred—turned grief into cover for their own agenda.

Des pressed close against my leg, catching the change in my mood. Around us, volunteers gathered the remnants, voices hushed.

Then Jason turned toward the memorial table. His face shifted—confusion, then shock.

"The box."

The table was bare but for the guest book, its pages lifting in the night breeze.

"Someone stole Grandpa's things," Callie whispered, strangled.

Des let out a low whine. The absence seemed to throb in the space where the box had been.

Jason pulled out his phone. "Constable McKay. I need to report a theft at the Echo Lake dock... during the lantern ceremony. Yes, I'll secure the scene."

The violation burned through me, sharp as winter air. Someone had orchestrated all of it—the intrusion, the chaos, even the fire—as cover for stealing Walter's memorial box.

But why? What could possibly be worth stealing from a dead man's effects?

CHAPTER THREE

The morning after felt hollowed out, like the space between thunder and lightning. I sat on the edge of the couch with Des pressed against my side, freshly showered but still feeling smoke-stained on the inside. My jacket from the night before hung over a chair, carrying the faint scent of woodsmoke and scorched fabric. Sleep had never really come. The restless energy that had carried me through the chaos at the dock hummed under my skin, a low vibration that coffee alone wouldn't settle.

The house was too quiet, even for a Sunday. The clock in the hallway ticked loudly and deliberately, each second reminding me that the world had moved forward into morning while I still felt caught in last night's ruin.

A soft knock broke the silence. Jason stood on the porch, weary but steady in a fresh uniform. The autumn light caught on the polished buttons of his RCMP jacket.

"Coffee?" he asked, stepping inside without waiting for an invitation.

"In the pot."

He moved through the kitchen with the comfort of someone who'd grown up in this house, pulling mugs from the same cupboard we'd raided as kids. Des padded after him, nails clicking against the floor, clearly hoping for a scrap of toast or at least a bit of attention. The smell of brewed coffee filled the room as Jason poured a mug and brought one to me.

The familiarity should have been soothing. Instead it felt like we were actors in a play, running through the motions of normal life while the stage set still smouldered in the wings.

"Any leads on the theft?" I asked.

Jason's jaw tightened. "Scene's processed. But you know how it is with thefts at public events—too many people, too much movement. No witnesses saw anyone near the memorial table during the disruption."

"What about Dawn's crew? They had cameras rolling."

"Already checked. Their footage shows the crowd reacting when the fire started, not the table. Nothing useful." He handed me my mug. "Officially, we're treating it as opportunistic theft during a disturbance."

The word officially hung in the air like smoke, curling around everything he wasn't saying.

The creak of the staircase broke the silence. Callie shuffled down in her pyjamas, hair wild, phone clutched in her hand like an extra limb. She flopped onto the armchair and immediately started scrolling.

"The blog comments are exploding," she said without looking up. "Dawn's followers are defending her. Half the locals say it was an honest mistake; half say she was set up."

"What about the theft?" I asked. "Are people talking about Dad's missing things?"

"Not much," she said, thumb flicking the screen. "Most of the chatter is about the lanterns and the fire. The actual theft barely registers."

Jason and I exchanged a look. The theft was being drowned out by the drama. Which might have been the point all along.

"What's your read on Dawn?" I asked Callie. "You follow her."

Callie hesitated, then shook her head. "She's too polished to make that kind of mistake. She does her homework. But maybe that's what someone wanted us to think."

"Meaning?"

"Meaning someone needed her there. Either as a distraction or as proof." Callie set her phone down and met my eyes. "Question is whether she was the target or just the weapon."

Before I could respond, footsteps sounded on the walk. A moment later, Bertha's voice carried through the door.

"Tilly? You decent?"

I opened the door to find her holding a casserole dish wrapped in a faded tea towel. The scent of baked macaroni rose through the cloth, rich with cheese and onions. She nodded to Jason and Callie as she came in, her sharp eyes taking in more than I wanted her to.

"How are you holding up?" she asked me.

"Fine."

"Hm." That single syllable carried sixty years of experience with people who said fine when they meant anything but. She set the dish on the counter with the weight of someone who had been bringing food to grieving families her whole life.

"Sit," she said. It wasn't a request.

When I did, she folded her hands. "I wanted you to hear this from me before the gossip mill twists it."

Here it came.

"Charlotte called an emergency council meeting for tomorrow morning. She's calling it damage control." Bertha's expression sharpened. "Funny thing, though—two days ago, she was asking pointed questions about the memorial setup.

What would be displayed, who had access, when it would be in place."

The coffee soured in my mouth. "She knew."

"Someone did." Bertha's tone stayed mild, but her eyes said otherwise. "And now she's spinning the whole thing as a misunderstanding. Proposing council oversight for all festival events—making the response the story instead of the disruption."

Jason straightened. "If she asked about the setup before it happened, that suggests premeditation."

"Can you prove it?" I asked.

He shook his head. "Not without a recording. It's all hearsay. Officially, I can only focus on the theft."

Bertha folded her arms, eyes narrowing. "Then here's what I don't understand—why steal Walter's things in the first place? The coin collection, sure. That's worth money, and it's the only reason the police can investigate at all. But the photos and papers? Who would want those?"

Jason didn't answer. He couldn't.

"Feels deliberate to me," Bertha went on. "People don't risk fire and chaos for some coins. Whoever took that box wanted something inside it."

Jason rubbed at his temple. "Maybe. But without evidence, I can't make that case. On paper it looks like a thief grabbed the most valuable item in reach."

"And you believe that?" she asked, sharp as a knife.

Jason hesitated, then glanced at me. "I believe someone planned this. But I can't prove it yet."

Bertha's mouth pressed thin. "Charlotte Bugle wouldn't move this fast unless she had something to hide. I've seen too many of their tricks to think otherwise. Whether she orchestrated it or just used it afterward—that's the part you'll have to figure out."

Her certainty made my chest tighten. She didn't know Walter was alive. She couldn't. But she knew the Bugles were dangerous, and that knowledge alone was enough to plant suspicion deep.

After she left, Jason paced to the window, tension in every line of his shoulders. "I hate this. There's so much I can't touch officially."

"Like what?"

"Like why Dad's effects were targeted. On the report, it's just opportunistic theft. But if someone went through his things looking for something specific…" He trailed off.

Callie wrapped her arms around herself. "What if they were?"

Jason looked grim. "That's what worries me."

The silence pressed down, filled only by the faint hum of the fridge and Des shifting at my feet.

"The disruption might've been politics," I said finally. "But stealing during the chaos? Either they were looking for something in Dad's papers, or they wanted to show us they could take whatever they pleased."

Jason met my eyes. "Be careful, Tilly. Whoever did this planned it carefully. They'll cover their tracks."

"Or deal with anyone who gets too close," Callie added.

The warning hung in the air. They wanted me to let it go, to fold myself back into the rhythm of normal life.

But someone had some of Dad's papers now. And that meant secrets we hadn't uncovered ourselves might already be in the wrong hands.

I stood, the decision already forming. "Come on. Festival prep won't wait. Callie and I promised Fern we'd help at the museum this morning."

Des's ears pricked as if she approved. The unease stayed, sharp and unrelenting, as I reached for my jacket.

That afternoon, Callie, Des, and I walked to the Balsam Bay Heritage Museum. Fern had asked for help setting up the Aurora Nights displays, and I needed something to focus on besides the morning's revelations about Charlotte's suspicious timing and the theft.

The museum had once been Samuel Melvin's house—Balsam Bay's founder, who hadn't believed in doing anything halfway. Three stories of Manitoba limestone and timber, built to outlast generations. My mother, Kathleen, had been its first curator when it opened to the public thirty years ago. Walking through these rooms always felt like stepping into her memory, seeing the careful way she'd arranged each display to tell our town's story.

Inside, the smell of old wood and preservation chemicals wrapped around us like a familiar coat. Des's nails clicked on the hardwood as she investigated the new arrangement of boxes and displays waiting to be assembled.

"Tilly!" Fern's voice carried from the back rooms. "Thank goodness. I'm drowning in geological samples and star charts."

We found her in what had been the original dining room, now converted to display space, half-buried in boxes and scattered materials. Sean's blue pickup was visible through the window, which explained the collection of rock samples spread across the long table—each one tagged with his precise handwriting.

"Sean's been incredible," Fern said, following my gaze. "He's been cataloguing specimens all week for the geological history display. People come here for the aurora, but we figured they should also see what makes this land so special—the ancient Shield rock beneath it all."

She gestured at the organized chaos surrounding her. "I

need to grab some coffee from the kitchen. This is going to take all afternoon. Want some?"

"We're good," I said, and Callie shook her head.

Fern disappeared through the back doorway just as footsteps approached from the main hall. Sean appeared carrying another wooden crate, rock dust on his jacket and that easy smile I'd grown accustomed to.

"Hey there," he said, setting down the crate with obvious care. "How are you holding up after yesterday?"

"We're managing." I watched him begin unpacking specimens, each movement was deliberate and careful. "That's quite a collection."

"Figured I'd bring some of the more interesting pieces. Really showcase what makes this area unique, geologically speaking." He held up a piece of banded iron formation, the layers catching the afternoon light. "Three billion years old, this one. Formed when the Earth's atmosphere first had oxygen."

His enthusiasm was genuine, infectious even. Whatever mysteries surrounded his contract work, his passion for rocks was unmistakably real.

"The festival's lucky to have your expertise," I said.

"This place has been good to me." He unwrapped another specimen, this one a cluster of clear crystals. "Amazing what you can find around here if you know where to look. The Shield runs right through this region—some of these formations are older than complex life on Earth."

Callie picked up one of his labels, reading it with interest. "Are you using any of this for your book research?"

"Some of it." Sean's phone buzzed. He glanced at it, and something flickered across his expression—there and gone. "The other project keeps me busy too, but there's always time for community work."

"Your mysterious employer still keeping you under wraps?" I kept my tone light, but I was curious about that momentary tension.

"Client confidentiality and all that." The easy smile returned, but something guarded lingered in his eyes. "Interesting work, though. Gets me out exploring places most people never see."

Before I could probe further, movement in the doorway caught my attention. Charlie stood there, rolling his shoulders like he'd been hauling boxes.

"Afternoon, everyone." His voice carried his usual helpful tone. "Thought you could use extra hands after yesterday's... difficulties."

He stepped into the room, stretching as if he'd just set something heavy down in the hall. His eyes flicked across the cases, the doorway, the archive hall—quick glances most people wouldn't have noticed. Des leaned against my leg, ears pricked.

"That's thoughtful, Charlie," I said evenly.

"We're all trying to pull together after what happened." He drifted toward Sean's table. "Incredible specimens. I didn't realize we had this kind of variety around here."

"Manitoba's full of surprises," Sean said, lifting another stone from its crate.

Charlie bent over a label, frowning as if he was puzzling out Sean's handwriting. "Some of these must be pretty fragile. Does Fern keep the more valuable ones in back?"

Sean smiled, still focused on his work. "She's careful with all of them. Some are sensitive to heat or light—takes chemistry knowledge to store them right."

Charlie nodded, filing that away. "Big responsibility." His tone was casual, but I caught his eyes slide toward the closed storage doors before he straightened.

"Fern does an amazing job," Sean said. "Though after yesterday, I imagine security's going to be a bigger concern."

"Speaking of yesterday," Charlie added a moment later, voice tinged with sympathy, "that theft must have been hard on top of everything else."

"It was," I said carefully.

He let the silence stretch, then shook his head. "Terrible, really. You never know if people are after money or…something else." The pause was just a hair too long, as though he wanted me to fill it in.

"The police are investigating," I said instead.

"Good. Jason's sharp. Just… a crowd like that? Hard to pick out what really happened."

He didn't push further, but the echo of his words stayed with me, sharper than anything in his expression.

Sean looked up from his work. "The whole memorial disruption was strange. Dawn Kessler doesn't strike me as someone who'd make that kind of mistake."

"Charlotte says it was a miscommunication," Charlie said quickly. "Someone gave Dawn wrong information about the memorial being a public festival event. These things happen when you're coordinating multiple venues and schedules."

"Charlotte seems to have everything well in hand now," I observed, watching his reaction.

Charlie's face brightened with obvious pride. "She really does. She's been working around the clock to make sure the festival goes smoothly. She really cares about this community."

"How long have you two been together?" Callie asked.

"Eight months." His expression softened into something genuinely tender. "She's amazing. So driven, so passionate about making Balsam Bay better. Sometimes people don't understand her methods, but her heart's absolutely in the right place."

The devotion in his voice was complete. Whatever Charlotte asked of him, he'd do it without question.

"It's nice that you support each other," I said carefully.

"We're a team," Charlie said with evident pride. "We both want what's best for the town. Sometimes that means making tough decisions that not everyone understands."

The echo of this morning's conversation made my stomach tighten. Tough decisions like orchestrating memorial disruptions? Like stealing from grieving families?

We worked for another hour, Charlie proving genuinely helpful with the physical labour of moving display cases and arranging specimens. But I couldn't shake the feeling that his real purpose was observation. He asked casual questions about museum security procedures, about who had keys, about whether there were cameras in the archive rooms. Each query was embedded in reasonable conversation, but the pattern was unmistakable.

Des never fully relaxed around him. When Charlie reached for one of Sean's more valuable specimens, she stepped forward—not aggressive, just deliberately placing herself between us. Charlie noticed, pulling his hand back with a nervous laugh.

"Your dog doesn't trust easily, does she?"

"She's a good judge of character," I said, keeping my tone light.

As we finished arranging the last display case, Fern returned with obvious satisfaction at our progress.

"This looks wonderful! Sean, your specimens are going to be the highlight of the geological display."

"Happy to contribute," Sean said, packing up his tools.

"And Charlie, thank you so much for your help," Fern added. "With everything that's happened, seeing people come together like this really helps."

"My pleasure." Charlie smiled, but his gaze swept the room one last time, lingering not on the displays but on the locks, the windows, the exits. A mental map, neat as a blueprint.

Walking home in the late afternoon light, Des trotting beside us with obvious relief to be away from the museum, I found myself more unsettled than when we'd arrived.

"You're too quiet," Callie observed. "What's wrong?"

"Charlie's questions about the theft. The way he kept probing about what was taken, whether we knew if someone was looking for something specific."

"Like he was trying to figure out if someone found what they were after?"

I nodded. "And all those questions about museum security, disguised as casual conversation."

"Mom," Callie said, her voice dropping. "Charlotte was asking about the memorial setup before it happened. Now Charlie's asking about what was taken after. It's like they're working through a checklist."

The thought chilled me more than the approaching evening. Not random opportunism but systematic planning. Charlotte gathering information beforehand, Charlie following up after, both of them probing to see what we knew, what we suspected.

"If they're still collecting information," I said slowly, "then yesterday wasn't the end of something."

"It was reconnaissance," Callie finished.

The theft hadn't been the goal. It had been a test, or perhaps just the first step. Someone had Dad's papers now, and they were still deciding what to do with what they'd found. Or worse—they hadn't found what they were looking for and were preparing to try again.

Des pressed against my leg as we walked, her watchful attention reminding me that threats didn't always announce themselves. Sometimes they came wearing helpful smiles and asking innocent questions, gathering information for purposes we couldn't yet understand.

Whatever Charlie and Charlotte were planning—if they were indeed planning—yesterday's memorial disruption had only been their opening move.

CHAPTER FOUR

The general store's coffee urn hissed as I topped it up. Callie and I had been running Dad's store for a few months now—well, with Bertha's steady hand keeping us from disaster. By this point, we knew who took cream, who took sugar, and which hockey debates would last until spring. I set out a fresh pitcher of cream for the two old-timers in the corner, already deep in their morning debate about the Jets' chances this year.

With the mugs refilled and peace temporarily restored, I made my way back behind the counter. Callie was perched on the tall stool, laptop open, her frown sharper than usual. Des stretched on the rug by the heater, tail thumping once when she saw me.

"Mom, you need to see this."

She turned the screen toward me. It was yesterday's blog post—her cheerful write-up about festival preparations and small-town energy—meant to shift attention away from Dad's memorial. Instead, the comments beneath it had grown like weeds overnight.

"They're worse this morning," Callie said, scrolling fast.

One line was highlighted in pale yellow: *Dawn seemed like she was genuinely trying to help. Funny how she ended up in exactly the right spot to cause the most trouble.*

The words prickled under my skin. "What's that supposed to mean?"

"No idea. But it's local—same IP range as several others."

She tapped another. *Some families think they own this town's grief. Maybe it's time for transparency.*

That one cut sharper, resentment wrapped in virtue.

"They're still going at it," Callie said, lowering her voice as the bell jingled and a man in a denim jacket came in for nails and a pack of jerky. "Two days later, and the arguments have only gotten worse. Outsiders defending Dawn, locals digging in. I thought it would fizzle by now, but it hasn't."

Before I could answer, the bell jangled again and a whirlwind swept in—Enid, Nora, and Trish, scarves flying, perfume arriving a full second before they did.

"Morning, girls!" Enid boomed, marching straight to the counter with a tin in her arms. "Mandy sent muffins for this fine Monday morning—said you'd need the energy with festival week ahead. Cranberry-orange. Baked before sunrise. Don't say we never look after you." She popped the lid with a flourish, releasing a wave of citrus and sugar into the store.

"Can you believe the talk?" Nora exclaimed, swinging her shopping bags dangerously close to a display of preserves. "Half the town swears that poor Dawn was innocent—"

"—and the other half," Trish broke in, gloves flapping as she gestured, "say she was planted. On purpose. Imagine! At Walter's memorial!"

"Which is nonsense," Enid said, though the sparkle in her eye suggested she was enjoying herself. She jabbed a finger toward Callie. "And now your little blog is fanning the flames."

Callie's blush rose fast. "That wasn't—"

"Supposed to be?" Trish's laugh rang out like wind chimes. "Oh, honey, nothing online is ever what it's supposed to be. Just wait until you post an oatmeal cookie recipe. There'll be a fistfight over raisins vs chocolate chips."

The three of them cackled, gathered their scarves, and swirled out the door as suddenly as they'd come. Their voices trailed down the street long after the bell stopped jangling.

Callie snapped her laptop shut, then rested both hands on the cover as if steadying herself. "I'm not going to let them turn this into gossip," she said, her voice low but steady. "My blog's about community, not clickbait. If I write about the disruption, I'll do it the right way—facts, context, no rumours. That's what I was trained for, and I'm not backing down now." The determined set of her shoulders looked less like a flustered daughter and more like the journalist she'd worked so hard to become.

She opened the laptop again, calmer this time, fingers hovering over the keys as though already sketching out her next post. Pride welled up in me—Callie wasn't shying away, she was claiming her responsibility. But pride has a way of carrying its shadow close behind, and mine came quick: if she was finding her footing, was I only stumbling through mine instead?

I leaned on the counter, letting the rhythms of the store wash over me—the squeak of floorboards, the till drawer sticking like always, the clink of jars as someone compared jams. Walter had built this place into a hub, and now it was my turn to keep it humming. Some days I managed. Other days, like now, I felt like I was only pretending to fill his shoes.

Des nudged her nose against my shin, as if to remind me I wasn't as alone as I felt.

The storeroom door creaked, and Bertha emerged, clipboard tucked under one arm and a box of preserves balanced on her hip. She set the box on the shelf with practiced efficiency, straightened three jars in a row, and came to the counter without missing a beat.

"Here," she said briskly, plopping a manila folder down. "Festival vendor payments. Don't lose it—unless you'd like me to scold you in front of the committee."

I raised a brow. "Wouldn't dare."

Bertha flicked her eyes toward Callie's laptop. "Blog's been lively."

"That's one word for it," Callie muttered.

"Mm." Bertha jotted something on her clipboard. "Publicity's like yeast—it makes things rise whether you want them to or not."

Callie gave a reluctant snort.

"Got a message from Charlotte. She's in a flap," she said crisply. "Reminded me of that committee meeting at eleven. Festival security's on the docket after the memorial business." She made a mark on her clipboard, then added dryly, "And of course, she wants one story, one voice, one tidy version for the visitors."

"Whose story?" I asked.

Bertha's mouth pinched. "Exactly. That's what they'll bicker about until somebody sensible cuts through."

"You should go," Callie murmured, catching the look on my face. "See what they're planning."

"My advice?" Bertha said as she restocked a pile of brochures, "Bring coffee to the meeting. Civil tongues dry up without it."

I lowered my voice. "Yesterday you said Charlotte had been poking around about the service. Has anyone else been asking pointed questions? Anything that might explain how Dawn knew to show up when she did?"

Bertha paused mid-scribble. "Not that I've heard. And if I had, they'd regret telling me." Her gaze flicked up, sharp. "What are you fishing for, Tilly?"

"Just covering bases."

"Hmph." She snapped her clipboard shut. "Well, if someone's stirring trouble, they've picked the wrong town. Eleven o'clock sharp—don't be late."

She marched back toward the storeroom, clipboard tucked tight against her side, already muttering about the syrup shipment.

The store settled back into its hum. A child pressed his nose against the candy jars, his mother calling him back. Des sighed and flopped onto her side. On the surface, ordinary. Underneath, tension thickened like the cool autumn air rolling through the open door.

Someone had steered Dawn into our grief. Someone had taken Dad's things. And now someone was twisting Callie's blog into a wedge. None of it felt accidental.

Callie closed her laptop with a little more force than necessary and looked at me, eyes suddenly steady. "I'm not going to let this turn into Dawn versus the town, or our family versus everyone else," she said. "But neither am I going to let lies spread just because they're convenient. I'll keep reporting—facts, context, who said what and when—but I'll be careful. No naming sources who don't want it. No posting speculation. If something needs to be private to protect people, I won't put it up for clicks. But if something's damning and true, I'll corral the evidence before I write." She took a breath. "There's a line between being useful and being cruel. I'm tired of people crossing it."

Her voice had an adult note in it that made me straighten in my stool. "How will you do that?" I asked.

She tapped the screen. "I'll do the basics—verify what I

can, offer people the chance to respond before I post, flag inflammatory comments, and put context up front. I'll explain why I'm writing what I'm writing, not just throw accusations. And if the committee wants a 'unified story,' I won't be their mouthpiece. But I'll listen if they have facts to share. This isn't about clicks. It's about truth, and the town deserves a version of it that doesn't destroy people in the process."

It felt like a small, solid answer to the question that had been hanging over both of us—how to tell the truth without tearing the town apart. Callie's shoulders relaxed a little, as though saying it out loud had steadied her.

"I'll go to the meeting," I said finally. "The committee might tell us what they're actually afraid of."

"Want me to come?" Callie asked.

"Better if you stay here. Keep watching the comments. If someone's sending messages through your blog, we need to know what they're saying." Her fingers hovered over the keyboard, already composing notes.

Des thumped her tail once—steady as a drumbeat.

I gathered Bertha's folder and scanned the store automatically—who stood where, who carried what, how the flow of shoppers moved in and out. Old SAR habits—impossible to turn off.

I told myself I wasn't investigating. Just observing. But the line between the two blurred a little more with every passing hour.

The committee meeting had been exactly what I'd expected—concerns about festival logistics, worries over visitor expectations, and Charlotte's careful emphasis on 'maintaining community reputation.' But it was the encounter afterward that left me feeling cornered.

I was walking Des along one of the quieter side streets, enjoying the crisp October air and the crunch of leaves underfoot, when I spotted Erwina Lynch approaching. She carried a covered casserole dish like an offering, wearing her most sympathetic expression. In small towns, unsolicited casseroles often came with unsolicited advice.

"Tilly, dear," she called, her voice carrying that tone people use when they mean to soften the blow of what comes next. "I was just thinking about you and thought you might appreciate something warm for supper."

Before I could answer, she pressed the warm dish into my arms: tuna noodle casserole—the same one she'd delivered to every crisis in town for decades.

"That's very thoughtful, Erwina."

"It's the least I can do, considering everything your family's endured." Her eyes shone with the kind of concern that felt, to me, more like curiosity. "First losing Walter so suddenly, and now this unfortunate business at the memorial..."

Her pause was calculated—an opening for me to explain myself.

"We're managing," I said carefully.

"Of course you are. The McKays have always been pillars of this community." Erwina shifted her casserole lid slightly, letting out another puff of baked-cheese steam. "Walter always knew when to let sleeping dogs lie. So wise about not stirring up unnecessary trouble."

The comparison landed heavily. She was suggesting that wisdom meant staying quiet, not pressing further.

"I saw that poor Dawn woman this morning," Erwina continued, lowering her voice. "She was crying, Tilly. Absolutely devastated. Apparently she's been getting awful messages online—people claiming she disrupted the service on purpose."

My chest tightened. Whatever Dawn's role had been, she was paying a price for it.

"She seemed genuinely confused," I admitted.

"Exactly! Which is why we all need to be careful about how we talk about it. The poor girl made an honest mistake, and now she's being crucified." Erwina adjusted her grip on her purse, the gesture that always meant she was about to deliver her main point. "Charlotte's been working day and night to smooth things over and make sure the festival isn't tarnished by gossip."

There it was—the real message. Charlotte was handling it. My role was to fall in line.

"I'm sure Charlotte's handling it well," I said neutrally.

"She is, but it's such a burden for her. Especially when some people keep asking questions that stir up more trouble." Erwina's tone stayed syrupy, but her eyes were sharp. "I know your family has been through so much, dear. The last thing the town needs is more upheaval. We're all counting on things going smoothly."

Her words settled on me like a heavy coat—not a threat, but a reminder that I was being watched.

"Of course," I said. "Everyone wants the festival to succeed."

"Exactly. And your daughter's blog is drawing so much attention!" Erwina smiled brightly. "That could be wonderful for Balsam Bay—if she *uses it wisely*. Young people sometimes don't realize how their words ripple. But if Callie keeps her posts focused on the positive—the charm of the town, the excitement of the festival—that would be such a gift for us all."

Another gentle redirection. Keep Callie's writing sunny. Don't let her probe.

Des spotted a spaniel across the street and lunged, nearly pulling me off balance. Erwina steadied me with a firm hand.

"Careful, dear. You don't want to take on more than you can handle." Her tone was sweet, but the words carried more weight than a tightened leash. "Sometimes it's better to focus on what we can control instead of chasing things that only upset us."

We were interrupted by Charlie coming up from the direction of the festival grounds, clipboard in hand. He looked flustered, his hair sticking up at the back and a pencil tucked behind his ear.

"Afternoon, ladies," he said, though his attention landed squarely on me. "Tilly, Charlotte wanted me to, uh, tell you—" He shuffled his notes, flipping a page. "She asked me to tell you that if you need help dealing with... outside interest... in the weekend's events, the committee's ready to help coordinate."

"Outside interest?"

"Media, uh, social media, that sort of thing." He glanced at Erwina, who gave him a small approving nod. "We want to make sure everyone's on the same page. You know, so no one gets the wrong idea."

The message was obvious: stick to the narrative.

"I appreciate the offer," I said, though I didn't.

Charlie brightened, relieved. "Good, good. And, uh, Charlotte mentioned—oh yes—Callie's blog." He squinted at his clipboard. "She thinks it'd be best if Callie worked with the committee, you know, to highlight the positive aspects of festival weekend. Her posts are getting attention, and that's great, but... alignment would really help."

He checked his clipboard twice, as though Charlotte's words might rearrange themselves if he didn't get them exactly right.

His handwriting was neat to the point of fussiness—every

letter pressed hard, the loops of his C's curling like he'd practiced them. Funny, the things people rehearse when they're trying to impress.

"So what you're saying," I asked, "is you want Callie to write what Charlotte approves of."

"Oh, no—no, not exactly." Charlie's ears went red. "Just... coordinated messaging, that's all. Everyone sharing the same version of things. Consistency." He shot another quick glance at Erwina, who gave the faintest smile.

"And," Charlie added, "Dawn wants to apologize to your family. She feels terrible and thinks it might heal things if you met face-to-face."

The suggestion felt like a setup—close the book on the disruption, a neat bow tied in public.

"I'll think about it," I said.

Erwina and Charlie exchanged a look that said my answer wasn't quite good enough.

"Well," Erwina said brightly, "I should let you get home with that casserole before it cools. Remember, dear—we're all here for you."

Supportive words, but they felt like surveillance.

After they left, I stood with Des and the casserole, watching the bustle of early preparations. Volunteers hauled tables off a flatbed, chalked out spaces on the street, and hammered plywood signs. A pair of kids darted underfoot, chasing each other around crates while their parents shouted half-hearted warnings. The cheerful noise of setup carried through town, but underneath the bright bustle, I could see the choreography of damage control—people positioning themselves, smoothing rough edges, ensuring questions were swept aside before they gained traction.

Everyone wanted me to let it go. To trust that Charlotte

and her allies were handling it. To keep my head down, smile, and let Callie's blog serve as a postcard instead of a probe.

But letting go meant accepting that someone had deliberately used Dawn to disrupt Walter's memorial. It meant letting the same people who now controlled the story decide which truths mattered.

As I shifted the casserole in my arms, I thought about Dad. He'd been deliberate, steady, wise about which fights were worth having. But he'd also taught me that when something smelled wrong, you didn't turn your nose away.

And everything about yesterday's disruption, today's pressure, and the sudden interest in Callie's blog smelled wrong.

In two days the festival would open, and the push to smile and cooperate would grow even heavier. But tonight, alone with Des and Erwina Lynch's well-intentioned casserole, I had to decide whether I could live with the weight of unasked questions.

The community was watching. They wanted harmony—cheerful coverage—a town that looked unshakable. But someone had used Dawn to strike at Dad's memory.

And until I knew who and why, I couldn't pretend everything was fine.

CHAPTER FIVE

Tuesday morning, and the festival grounds buzzed with energy. It was the last full day before things officially began, and though I'd come early to help with the astronomy display, I found myself drawn to the human drama unfolding across the grounds.

Dawn Kessler moved through the crowd like a heat-seeking missile, her recorder and notebook were constant companions. What I'd initially mistaken for professional thoroughness now looked different in the harsh morning light. Relentless. Calculating. Like she'd already written the ending and was just collecting supporting quotes.

"So when you say the memorial disruption was 'unexpected,'" Dawn was saying to Mrs. Patterson, "what exactly do you mean by that? Had there been fractures brewing beforehand?"

Mrs. Patterson shifted uncomfortably. "Well, I wouldn't say tensions exactly—"

"But there must have been some underlying currents," Dawn pressed, pen poised. "Family conflicts? Political disagreements? Something that made the moment so... explosive?"

The word explosive hung in the air with uncomfortable weight. Mrs. Patterson mumbled something about needing to check on the book sale table and hurried away.

Dawn immediately pivoted to her next target—Joe Charles, who was carrying astronomy equipment toward Fern's display area.

"It's Joe, right? I'm Dawn Kessler from Canadian Cosmic Conversations. I understand you were a close friend of Walter McKay's. I'd love to get your perspective on the memorial service. As someone who knew Walter well, how did it feel when things went sideways?"

Joe paused, adjusted his grip on the telescope case, eyes fixed ahead. "Feels wrong," he said quietly.

"It felt wrong how? Like someone had planned it? Like there were people who wanted to disrupt the ceremony?"

"Feels wrong to be talking about it for entertainment." His voice carried a sharp edge I'd rarely heard from him. He continued walking without another word.

But Dawn wasn't deterred. She made a quick note into her recorder—something about 'community resistance to transparency'—then scanned the crowd for her next interview opportunity.

I watched the crowd dynamics shift around Dawn—the same way hikers unconsciously avoid unstable ground. People sensed danger without fully understanding why.

From my position near the aurora viewing schedule booth, I saw her corner Mandy near the food truck permits station. Even from a distance, I could see her leaning forward with that same aggressive energy, her questions coming rapid-fire as Mandy shifted from foot to foot.

"The thing about small communities," Dawn's voice carried on the morning breeze, "is that everyone knows everyone's business. So when something like this happens, people usually have theories about who might be behind it…"

Des pressed against my leg—a low rumble in her throat I felt more than heard. Her tail flicked once, ears angled sharply toward Dawn. My dog had always been good at reading situations, and right now her instincts were telling her something I was beginning to feel myself.

Dawn wasn't investigating the memorial disruption. She was feeding on it.

"Mom!" Callie appeared at my elbow, slightly breathless. "Have you seen what Dawn's doing?"

"Unfortunately."

"She's been at it since sunrise. Nora said Dawn knocked on her door at seven asking about 'community power structures' and whether there were any 'feuds or rivalries' that might explain what happened at the memorial."

I turned to watch Dawn approach Charlie, who was helping Fern arrange Sean's rock samples. Even Charlie's perpetual eagerness to please seemed strained as Dawn launched into an interrogation disguised as friendly conversation.

"Charlie, as someone close to the festival organizing committee, you must have insights into the local fault lines. When the memorial service went off-script, what was your immediate thought about who might have orchestrated it?"

Charlie glanced nervously toward Charlotte, who was across the field deep in conversation with the mayor. "I… I don't think anyone orchestrated anything. Sometimes things just go wrong."

"But you were there. You saw how it unfolded. The timing, the way it escalated—that doesn't happen randomly.

Someone had to have inside information about the ceremony plans."

"Dawn's questions aren't random either," Callie said quietly, her journalism training evident in her analysis. "She's building a narrative. The disrupted memorial isn't just background for her festival story—it's her story. She's decided what happened and now she's collecting quotes to support it instead of investigating objectively."

I watched Dawn pull out her phone, apparently recording Charlie's increasingly uncomfortable responses. The gleam in her eyes was unmistakable as she pressed for details about committee tensions and family dynamics. This wasn't journalism. This was opportunism.

"She's turned our family's pain into content," I said, the realization settling in me the way a bad map did—leading you somewhere you shouldn't go.

"And she's doing it badly," Callie added, her voice tight with professional irritation. "Leading questions, pressure tactics, fishing for predetermined narratives—that's not journalism, that's tabloid sensationalism. Any first-year journalism student would know better."

Callie adjusted the strap of her camera bag, the gesture tight with restrained energy.

"Mom." Callie's voice carried a warning I knew too well. "Look."

Dawn had moved on to Sean, who'd arrived with a load of equipment for the geology demonstration. She was showing him her notebook—pages of notes, from the looks of it. Sean's expression grew increasingly tense as he read, his jaw tightening with each line.

"Those aren't just interview notes," Callie said. "She's got research. Background information. Stuff she didn't get from this morning's fishing expedition."

I moved closer, Des trotting beside me with alert ears. The conversation fragments I caught made my blood run cold.

"—really important to get the full picture of community dynamics," Dawn was saying. "Charlotte mentioned there've been some interesting developments with land use discussions? Mining interests versus environmental protection?"

Sean's face had gone carefully blank—the expression he wore when he processed information he didn't want to share. "I'm not sure what Charlotte told you, but—"

"Oh, she was very helpful about the broader context. Economic pressures, outside interests, the way old families sometimes resist change. And Charlie provided some fascinating details about the museum's mineral collection and how that connects to local geological surveys."

Charlie had been feeding her information. Sean's geological work, museum holdings, community politics—all of it apparently fair game for Dawn's "compelling storytelling."

"The thing is," Dawn continued, her voice taking on a confidential tone, "I think someone deliberately disrupted that memorial service. And I think it connects to larger tensions in this community that people don't want to acknowledge."

Sean stepped back, his expression hardening. "You should be careful about making accusations without evidence."

"Oh, I'm not making accusations. I'm just following the story wherever it leads. And right now, it's leading to some very interesting questions about who benefits from keeping certain information buried."

The casual cruelty of that phrase—'keeping certain information buried'—in the context of Dad's memorial made my hands clench into fists. Dawn wasn't just exploiting our grief; she was weaponizing it.

Des gave a soft growl, sensing my rising anger. Around the festival grounds, other volunteers had begun to notice the pattern of Dawn's aggressive questioning. Conversations grew quieter when she approached. People started finding excuses to slip away whenever she appeared with her recorder.

But Dawn seemed energized by the resistance. She made notes about "community defensiveness" and "suspicious reluctance to discuss recent events." Every attempt to sidestep her questions became proof of the story she was already writing.

"She's treating this like we're all suspects in some conspiracy," Callie said, watching Dawn corner another volunteer near the first aid station. "And the worst part is, people are starting to believe her."

I could see it happening. The way conversations stopped when Dawn appeared. The nervous glances exchanged between committee members. The growing sense that something darker than grief and confusion was driving the questions being asked.

Dawn had arrived as a travel blogger documenting small-town festivals. But somewhere between the committee meeting and this morning's interrogation session, she'd become something else entirely: a predator who'd scented blood in the water and decided our family's tragedy would make for compelling content.

"We need to stop this," I said quietly.

"How? She's not doing anything technically wrong. Just asking questions."

But the questions themselves were the weapon. Each one designed to plant seeds of suspicion, to fracture the community solidarity that had rallied around our family, to transform a memorial service disruption into evidence of deeper conflicts and hidden agendas.

I watched Dawn approach Fern, adjusting the UV light over

a display of fluorescent minerals. Even sweet, trusting Fern looked uncomfortable as Dawn's questions began.

"Fern, I understand you have the potential to become quite the local celebrity with the science presentations you have planned. That must create some interesting dynamics with other committee members..."

Enough. I wasn't going to stand by while she hollowed out our grief for clicks. I turned toward the door. Des padded after me, ears still angled in warning.

I waited until the festival grounds cleared for lunch break, then followed Dawn toward the campground. She'd set up her travel trailer in a prime spot near the lake—with a direct view of the memorial site where the lantern ceremony had taken place.

The irony wasn't lost on me.

Dawn was sitting at her outdoor table, laptop open, transcribing interviews when I approached. She looked up with that same bright professional smile she'd been wearing all morning.

"Tilly! Perfect timing. I was hoping to get your perspective on—"

"We need to talk."

Something in my tone made her expression shift, though her smile stayed pinned in place.

"Of course. Would you like to sit down? I was just reviewing some fascinating information about community dynamics here in Balsam Bay."

"I'll stand." Des positioned herself beside me—alert and protective. "What exactly do you think you're doing?"

"I'm sorry?"

"This morning. The interrogations. The fishing for conflict and conspiracy theories. What's your actual agenda here?"

Dawn's laugh was light, carefully modulated. "I'm a journalist, Tilly. I ask questions. That's literally my job."

"Your job was supposed to be documenting the Aurora Festival. Not exploiting my family's grief for content."

"I understand you're upset about the ceremony, but—"

"You claimed to be concerned after what happened at the memorial. Today you're treating it like the best thing that ever happened to your story."

Dawn closed her laptop slowly, the professional mask slipping slightly. "Look, I didn't plan for the memorial service to go sideways. But when something newsworthy happens, I'm not going to pretend otherwise."

"Newsworthy." The word tasted bitter. "A family mourning their father is newsworthy to you?"

"A community disruption that reveals underlying tensions and potential conflicts of interest? Yes—absolutely." Dawn's voice carried a harder edge now, the friendly podcaster persona dropping away. "You might prefer everyone pretend nothing happened, but that's not how real journalism works."

"Real journalism?" I stepped closer, Des moving with me. "You've spent the morning pressuring people for gossip, making wild accusations, and turning a moment of grief into a conspiracy theory. That's not journalism. That's ambulance chasing."

Dawn stood, notebook clutched against her chest like armour. "I haven't made accusations. I've asked legitimate questions. If that makes people uncomfortable, maybe they should ask themselves why."

"Maybe they're uncomfortable because you're treating their neighbours like suspects and their community like a crime scene."

"Or maybe they're uncomfortable because there really is something going on here that people want to keep hidden." Dawn's eyes glittered. "The memorial disruption, the defensive community response, the way people clam up when I ask about local politics or land use. It's all connected, isn't it?"

"Connected to what?"

"That's what I'm trying to find out. But the more resistance I encounter, the more convinced I become that someone orchestrated Saturday's events for reasons that go deeper than poor judgment."

I stared at her, finally understanding. Dawn wasn't just exploiting the disruption—she genuinely believed she was uncovering a scandal. Our community's instinct for privacy and healing had been twisted in her mind into evidence of a cover-up.

"So you're looking for the deeper story—the why behind it all," I said.

"I think someone used it as an opportunity to send a message. About land rights, or development pressures, or family conflicts. Something big enough that people were willing to close ranks to protect it."

"And you think digging into it, regardless of who gets hurt, is your responsibility as a journalist."

"I think the truth is more important than protecting people's comfort."

"Even if there isn't a truth to uncover? Even if you're wrong?"

"Then the investigation will prove that, won't it?"

Investigation. She was treating our town like a case to be solved, our neighbours like evidence to be gathered.

"Let me be very clear." My voice dropped to the tone I'd used in SAR situations when lives were at stake. "Whatever you think you're investigating, you're going to stop. Today."

Dawn's eyebrows rose. "I'm sorry, but you don't get to tell me how to do my job. This is a free country."

"And I have every right to protect my family and community from someone who's decided our grief is grist for her content mill."

"Is that a threat?"

"It's a warning. Back off."

Dawn smiled, but there was nothing friendly in it. "You know what this conversation tells me? That I'm on the right track. The more defensive people get, the more certain I become there's something here worth defending."

She was right about one thing—my defensiveness only fed her suspicions. But I couldn't stand here and let her weaponize our pain.

"You want a story?" I said. "Here's one: Science and travel blogger comes to a small town, exploits family tragedy for content, destroys community trust for podcast ratings."

"Or," Dawn countered, "former SAR worker returns home just after her father disappears in a canoe accident, and when a journalist starts asking questions about a disrupted memorial, she shows up making threats. Which version do you think my audience will find more interesting?"

The threat was implicit but clear: cross me, and I'll make you part of the story.

"We're done here," I said.

"For now," she replied, already reaching for her laptop. "But I'll be around. Asking questions. Following leads. The story's not going away just because you want it to."

I walked back toward town with Des trotting beside me, my mind racing. Dawn wasn't going to stop. If anything, she'd double down.

The RCMP was investigating—but not the disruption. Jason had explained the scope clearly: the missing memorial box, the coin collection, the parts of the case that carried official weight. But the heart of it—the humiliation at the service, the way someone had hijacked Dad's memorial—that wasn't on their docket. And I knew better than to ask Jason to push when the police line had already been set.

The committee couldn't ban Dawn without creating a bigger scene. And Dawn had made it clear she'd keep pressing until she found whatever "truth" she was convinced was buried here.

Which left me with a choice: let her tear apart my community—or find out who really disrupted the memorial before she destroyed more lives with her theories.

I found Callie at Mandy's, scrolling through her blog comments while picking at a sandwich, a large mug of coffee in front of her—one of Mandy's mismatched cups from her collection that Callie had claimed as her favourite.

"How bad is it?" I asked.

"Getting worse by the hour. People are repeating Dawn's theories, adding their own. It's spinning out of control. And she's not even verifying—she's just amplifying speculation. It's irresponsible journalism."

"I know. I just talked to her. She's convinced the disruption was deliberate."

Callie set down her sandwich and lowered her voice. "Aren't we hiding something, though? Something she might stumble across?"

Dad's situation pressed at the back of my mind: the missing memorial box, the secret of his survival. "We are," I admitted. "And that alone is reason enough to keep her from digging deeper."

"But what if she's right? What if someone really did orchestrate the memorial disruption?"

"Then we need to find out who and why before she does.

Because whatever their motive, it'll be more complicated than the scandal she's spinning. And if she stumbles onto your grandfather being alive while chasing shadows…"

"She won't," Callie said firmly. "We won't let her."

I looked at her across the table. "I'll do my own investigating," I said, the decision crystallizing. "Not because Dawn forced me, but because someone violated our grief and they're going to answer for it."

"So we're really doing this again? Playing detective?"

"Not playing. Doing. Because if we don't, Dawn's version of the truth will be the only one left standing."

I thought about her threat to make me part of her story, about the neighbours she'd cornered, about the way she'd twisted Dad's memorial into "evidence."

"Someone orchestrated the disruption," I said. "The question is whether they did it to hurt our family, to send a message, or for reasons we haven't yet imagined. But we'll find out first. We'll find the real answer."

Callie's expression steadied. "Then I'm with you."

We talked it through, names surfacing as they came—people who'd been nearby, and those who'd been absent, people with reasons to care how the memorial played out. It wasn't much, but it gave us somewhere to start.

I looked around Mandy's cozy café. Dawn saw conspiracy and cover-ups. I saw neighbours trading gossip over pie, teenagers leaning across booths with milkshakes, Mandy bustling between tables with that quick laugh of hers. People trying to live their lives without having every word twisted into 'evidence.' This was my community. My home. And I wasn't going to let Dawn tear it apart.

"We find out who disrupted the memorial and why," I said. "Before Dawn does. And we make sure the truth doesn't destroy the community Dad loved."

Callie smiled faintly. "Then we're really doing this."

"We're really doing this."

Des stretched, then fell into step beside us as we headed home—her presence steady and reassuring. For the first time since Dawn Kessler had arrived, I felt like I was moving forward instead of reacting. Dawn wanted a story? Fine. But she was going to get the real one.

CHAPTER SIX

Wednesday afternoon's sun illuminated the downtown green space, which had transformed overnight. Hundreds of coloured lanterns hung ready among the old bur oaks, their intricate designs catching the light and hinting at the magic they'd create once evening fell. Children ran between clusters of astronomy enthusiasts who were already setting up telescopes, their chatter blending with Métis fiddle music drifting from the wooden bandstand.

I stood with Des at the edge of the growing crowd, watching our small community become something larger than itself. Tourists clustered around the information booth, clutching festival maps and discussing optimal viewing spots with genuine excitement. Charter buses were parked near the community centre, their passengers streaming out with cameras and eager faces.

Des had become an instant festival celebrity. Someone had given her an aurora-themed bandana that perfectly matched her new role as the festival mascot. Tourists formed lines for photos, and every few minutes, another family approached with smartphones held out hopefully.

"She's going to be more famous than any of us," I said to Callie, who appeared beside me with her tablet, fingers flying as she documented everything.

"Already is. The #BalsamBayDes hashtag is trending across Manitoba," Callie said, never looking up from her screen. "We've got tourism buses arriving from Winnipeg, people driving from Saskatchewan, even some folks who flew in from Toronto."

The scent of frying bannock and savoury hand pies mixed with the crisp autumn air, creating that perfect festival atmosphere. Local families moved with easy confidence, claiming prime spots for evening aurora viewing and greeting neighbours they hadn't seen since the last community gathering.

Across the green, two very different versions of the festival were playing out. Charlotte directed the setup with military precision, her clipboard never leaving her side and volunteers jumping to follow her colour-coded system. Her station featured professional displays, official brochures, volunteer assignments, and promotional materials that had clearly cost significant money. She looked every inch the successful event coordinator in her Aurora Nights jacket and official pin.

But twenty metres away, Fern's astronomy booth was attracting serious crowds despite the daylight hours. Her telescope remained carefully covered, but the informational posters she'd created drew science enthusiasts like magnets. She'd found her element: crouched down explaining star charts to wide-eyed children one moment, then answering complex questions about solar wind interactions from a University of Manitoba professor the next.

"The Indigenous peoples of this region have their own

aurora legends," Fern was saying to a captivated group who'd formed a semicircle around her display. "Stories about spirit dances and messages from ancestors dancing across the sky. It's a reminder that we're not the first to find magic in these lights—and that science and wonder aren't opposites."

Dawn appeared at the edge of the crowd, recorder in hand, quietly documenting Fern's teaching. Several tourists leaned closer, phones capturing not just Fern's words but the enthusiasm that made complex science accessible.

"Can you really see the lights dance?" a small child asked, eyes wide.

"Just wait until tonight," Fern promised, her whole face lit up. "I'll show you exactly where to look, and you'll see magic happen right above your head."

The crowd dynamics were impossible to miss. Every person who bypassed Charlotte's elaborate information station to join Fern's growing audience seemed to represent a personal slight. Charlotte's smile grew increasingly tight, her fingers finding her clipboard with sharp precision, knuckles whitening as she gripped it.

When Fern mentioned her Thursday evening astronomy session, Dawn immediately perked up with professional interest.

"That sounds incredible for the podcast," Dawn said, moving closer with her recorder. "Would you mind if I documented it?"

Charlotte's expression hardened as she watched Dawn gravitate toward Fern rather than seeking her approval first. The careful control she'd maintained over Dawn's access to community members was slipping.

But then Charlie appeared at Charlotte's elbow, clipboard in hand, looking flustered but eager to help. I watched as he immediately began redirecting tourists toward Charlotte's booth, his helpful manner masking what was obviously strategic positioning. When a reporter approached Fern directly, Charlie smoothly intervened.

"Any media requests need to go through Charlotte," he told the reporter, his tone friendly but firm. "She'll set up a proper interview slot."

The reporter frowned. "I only wanted a quick quote about viewing techniques."

"Charlotte will coordinate everything properly," Charlie assured him, steering him toward Charlotte's station.

Fern's shoulders dropped as the opportunity slipped past. She recovered quickly, turning back to the crowd of children waiting for a lesson on constellations. But the damage was done.

Des, who'd been enjoying her celebrity status, suddenly tensed beside me. Her ears pricked forward, and she stepped closer to my leg as Charlie passed nearby with his clipboard. She didn't growl or show obvious aggression, but her body language shifted—alert, watchful, protective. The change was subtle but unmistakable.

"Easy, girl," I murmured, running my hand along her head. Des stayed pressed against my side, her attention tracking Charlie's movements through the crowd.

Meanwhile, Charlotte held court beneath her canopy like a general in the field. She glanced over every few minutes to check crowd positioning, and when tourists strayed toward Fern or toward Dawn's recorder, her lips tightened into a smile not meant for photographs.

"Mom, look at this."

Callie thrust her tablet toward me.

The comments were short, deliberate—like someone whispering through keyholes.

Ask what was really in the box.

The memorial wasn't what it seemed.

Some secrets should stay buried.

"Those aren't tourists," I said, reading them again. "They're local. They know too much."

Callie's jaw tightened. "It feels like someone's using my blog to pass notes."

I watched Charlotte's brittle control across the festival grounds, noted Charlie's constant information gathering disguised as helpfulness, saw the way Dawn was building her narrative by collecting fragments from different sources. Someone was feeding the flames of suspicion, using Callie's growing platform to fan doubt about what had really happened at Dad's memorial.

The festival swirled around us—laughter, music, the excited chatter of visitors discovering our small town's magic. But underneath the celebration, I could feel the careful choreography of damage control—the positioning and manoeuvring that had started the moment Dawn arrived with her recorder and questions.

Des stayed close, her steady presence anchoring me as I watched the carefully orchestrated chaos. Someone was using the festival's success to create divisions none of us anticipated.

Time to start asking the right questions.

I waited for a lull in traffic around Charlotte's booth, watching as the last family wandered off with their official festival maps and colour-coded schedules. The afternoon crowd had thinned slightly, giving me the opening I needed.

Des positioned herself strategically beside me, her attention focused not on the passing tourists but on Charlotte's station. Her ears remained alert, her body language suggesting she was reading the mood of everyone in our vicinity. Whatever she sensed, it kept her close to my side.

I took a breath, preparing my approach. Be direct but not accusatory. Ask questions that revealed information without putting Charlotte entirely on the defensive. Though given her territorial behaviour all day, that might be impossible.

Charlotte looked up as I approached, her professional smile sliding into place with practiced ease. She straightened her jacket and gripped her clipboard like a shield.

"Tilly! How wonderful that you're finally getting a chance to enjoy the festival. I hope you're impressed with what we've accomplished here."

"Charlotte, I need to understand how Dawn knew about the memorial timing."

The smile faltered for just a moment before reforming, tighter this time. "I tried to control her access, Tilly. She was remarkably persistent."

"The ceremony was by invitation only. How did Dawn know where and when?" I kept my voice level, matter-of-fact.

Charlotte's fingers drummed against her clipboard. "She asked everyone, Tilly. You can't control a journalist determined to dig up information. I've been protecting this festival from people like her for weeks."

"Who else knew the specific details? The timing, the location?"

"Committee members. Church staff." Charlotte's response was too quick, too rehearsed. "It's not as if it was some state secret."

"Did you discuss the memorial with Dawn directly?"

Charlotte hesitated—just for a beat. "She was asking everyone questions, pushing for details. I may have mentioned that there was a private ceremony planned for after the church memorial."

"You were there when Dawn showed up. You saw how shocked she looked when you told her it was private."

"People can fake surprise, Tilly." The comment was sharp, calculated. "Journalists are skilled at manipulating situations for maximum impact."

That felt like deflection. "Did you contact Bertha about the arrangements? She mentioned someone from the committee had questions about logistics."

Another hesitation. Charlotte's eyes flicked away before meeting mine again. "I... yes, I may have called to confirm some details. To ensure everything went smoothly for your family."

There it was. Charlotte had insider knowledge and had been in contact with Bertha about the memorial plans. The pieces were there, but something about her manner suggested she was holding back more than she was revealing.

Charlotte seemed to realize she'd revealed too much, because she immediately went on the offensive. "You know, Tilly, I understand you're upset about what happened, but perhaps we should focus on moving forward. The festival is what matters now."

"Some people don't respect boundaries," Charlotte continued, the irony of her statement apparently lost on her. "Dawn showed up uninvited, disrupted a private family moment, and now she's using it as content for her podcast. It's unconscionable."

Then Charlotte's tone shifted, carrying an edge that made me step back. "Maybe some disruptions serve a purpose."

"What do you mean by that?"

Charlotte was already backtracking. "I just mean that sometimes these things happen for a reason. Perhaps it's time to let the past rest and focus on the future of our community."

The manipulation was subtle but unmistakable. "Your

father would want you to focus on healing, not investigating," she said, her voice adopting a falsely gentle tone.

Before I could respond, Charlie appeared at Charlotte's elbow with what he claimed was an "urgent" volunteer question.

"Charlotte, we need to coordinate the evening setup," he said, slightly out of breath, as if he'd been running. "The sound system volunteers need direction, and there's a question about parking overflow."

Charlotte glanced at him with mild irritation. "Can't this wait five minutes?"

"Of course," Charlie said, but instead of leaving, he lingered awkwardly. "Sorry, I couldn't help overhearing. You're talking about what happened at the memorial service?"

"We were all there when it happened," he continued, jumping into the conversation uninvited. "Saw the whole thing. Dawn looked genuinely shocked when Charlotte told her it was private." The way he volunteered the information felt too eager, too defensive.

Charlie nodded earnestly. "Charlotte's always emphasizing community responsibility. We were both focused on making sure everything ran smoothly for your family."

"I'd be happy to help you coordinate information, Tilly," Charlie added, his helpful manner more invasive than supportive. "Make sure you get accurate details about who was where and when."

That's when Des growled.

It was soft, barely audible, but unmistakable. I'd heard her make that sound before—not aggressive, but warning. Her body tensed beside me, her attention fixed entirely on Charlie.

"Des," I murmured, placing a hand on her head. She quieted but remained alert, as if something about Charlie triggered an instinct I should trust.

Charlie's smile wavered. "Your dog seems... unsettled."

"She's a good judge of character," I said, echoing what I'd told him at the museum.

I made mental notes as the conversation wound down: Charlotte had motive—controlling the festival narrative. She had knowledge—she'd spoken with Bertha about memorial logistics. But she'd also been there when Dawn arrived, had seen Dawn's apparent shock at learning it was private. If Charlotte had fed Dawn the information, why the elaborate performance?

Something was off about their coordination. Charlie's too-eager defence of Charlotte's innocence felt rehearsed. I needed to verify their stories with other sources, needed to understand who really gave Dawn those "specific details" she'd mentioned.

"Well," Charlotte said, her professional mask sliding back into place, "I hope that clears things up. Now, if you'll excuse me, there are still festival preparations to oversee."

As I walked away with Des, I couldn't shake the feeling that Charlotte was hiding something important. Her responses had been too careful, too practiced. Whether she'd directly caused the disruption or simply failed to prevent it, she knew more than she was telling.

And Charlie's sudden appearance, his eager helpfulness and Des's instinctive warning suggested the web of deception around that memorial ran deeper than I'd initially suspected.

CHAPTER SEVEN

After my encounter with Charlotte, I needed to talk with someone who might be more forthcoming. Yesterday, Fern had seemed nervous when Dawn was asking questions—as though she knew something she wasn't ready to share. In my SAR days, that kind of nervousness usually meant someone was struggling with information they felt they shouldn't reveal.

"I think I'll stop by the museum," I told Des, who was still pressed against my leg after Charlie had passed by with his clipboard. Her reaction to him was becoming impossible to ignore - alert, protective, wary. Des had excellent instincts about people.

What did I actually know about Fern? Museum volunteer for two years; astronomy enthusiast; quiet—until she'd suddenly blossomed into a confident science communicator. She'd mentioned university astronomy courses, but her knowledge seemed deeper than amateur level. And her nervousness around Charlotte's control felt genuine, not calculated.

"Come on, girl. Maybe Fern will have some insights about what's been happening."

We walked away from the festival crowds, Des trotting beside me with obvious relief to be leaving the noise behind. The afternoon sun slanted between the trees as we headed toward the museum's familiar brick façade.

But I was focused on inconsistencies now. Fern's expertise versus her claimed amateur status. Charlotte's need to control Dawn's access to community members. Charlie's helpful manner that felt like surveillance.

Des padded beside me, no longer torn between the festival's excitement and protective duty.

The museum felt cool and quiet after the bustling energy of the festival grounds. Late afternoon light filtered through the tall windows, casting long shadows across the polished floors. I found Fern in the geology section, carefully arranging Sean's mineral specimens in a display case that caught the light like captured rainbows in a glass.

"These specimens are stunning," I said, genuinely impressed. "I never realized we had such geological complexity here."

"Manitoba holds more surprises than most people expect," Fern agreed, lifting a piece of striated quartz with practiced care. "Everyone pictures endless prairies, but the Canadian Shield cuts right through this region."

Her knowledge impressed me, and I found myself genuinely curious about the stories these ancient stones could tell. I remembered helping my mother arrange displays like this when I was young, listening to her explain the significance of each piece.

"Your mother was Kathleen McKay, wasn't she?" Fern's voice carried reverence. "I've heard she practically built this museum from nothing."

"She did." The familiar weight settled in my chest. "Years of collecting donations, cataloguing everything, developing educational programs. She used to say the museum was the town's memory keeper."

We continued arranging the displays, working in comfortable quiet. As I moved around the geology section, I noticed a smaller display area tucked near the back - not part of Sean's formal collection, but a hodgepodge of local artifacts and donated items. Old farming tools, faded photographs, a collection of buttons, and various odds and ends that seemed to embody the town's accumulated history.

A rough chunk of dark rock sat among Sam Melvin's old surveying equipment—looking oddly out of place among the brass instruments and leather-bound notebooks.

"Why is this here?" I wondered aloud, picking up the unremarkable stone. When I turned it over, I found a clear "K" carved into one face.

K. For Kathleen? Could it be one of Mom's little jokes? She'd always had a quirky sense of humour about her displays. But it seemed so random, sitting here with Sam's things. Just an old rock with a letter scratched into it—probably nothing more than that.

I shrugged and set it back where I'd found it, dismissing the thought. There were more pressing mysteries to solve.

"Fern, I need to ask about the lantern ceremony. It was beautiful. The lanterns you and your volunteers set up made it especially memorable."

Her face brightened slightly. "Thank you. We worked hard to make everything perfect for your family." Then her expression grew troubled. "Until..."

"Until Dawn showed up," I finished. "Did you know Dawn before she arrived in town?"

"Only through her podcast." A flush coloured her cheeks. "I'm a fan, actually - I've been following her work for months. She's a wonderful storyteller, so it's been amazing to work with her."

The enthusiasm seemed genuine, but there was something underneath it. A carefulness in how she spoke about Dawn.

"Dawn seemed to know quite a bit about our community for someone who just arrived," I said, watching Fern's reaction carefully.

Fern's cheeks flushed again. "I'm sorry," she said, bowing her head. "She asked me about the memorial timing. She seemed to know a lot about it already, and I thought it was public information, so I told her the location." Her voice grew smaller. "I didn't mean any harm."

There it was. The source of her nervousness.

"What exactly did Dawn ask you?"

"She said she wanted to document authentic grief—how small communities honour their lost members." Fern was fidgeting with the display now, moving specimens that didn't need moving. "I thought it sounded respectful. Educational."

But Dawn had deliberately sought out that information. Not stumbled across it, not overheard it—actively gathered intelligence about a private memorial service.

"Charlotte must have been upset when she found out," I said carefully.

Fern's shoulders tensed. "Charlotte said I should have directed everything through her. That Dawn was taking advantage of my..." She paused, looking for the word. "Naivety."

"Is that what Charlotte called it?"

"Among other things." Fern's voice was barely audible. "She was angry about me giving Dawn information without permission. Said it made the entire festival committee look unprofessional."

Des had positioned herself near the entrance, her protective instincts heightened by the tension in our conversation. Fern noticed her alert stance, and looked more troubled.

"I really thought Dawn understood our community values. When she talked about documenting authentic stories..." Fern trailed off, looking distressed. "I should have been more careful about what information I shared."

The hurt in her voice was genuine. Whatever else Fern might be hiding, her guilt about the situation was real.

"Dawn's very good at what she does," I said carefully. "I'm sure she didn't mean for things to go wrong like they did."

"No, of course not. She was horrified when she realized what had happened." Fern's loyalty to Dawn was still intact, even through her distress. "But I still should have checked with Charlotte before telling her anything. I feel terrible about my part in ruining your family's ceremony."

"I just need to be more careful moving forward," she added quickly. "The lighting for tomorrow night's stargazing event needs to be perfect—and—" She stopped abruptly, as if catching herself before revealing something. "Well, Arlo thinks the positioning should be different, but I'm not sure..."

"Arlo had thoughts about the lighting setup?"

Fern's cheeks reddened. "He's been helping me with the technical setup. The lights for the evening programs can be finicky." She busied herself with unnecessary adjustments to the display. "Just coordination details."

But her obvious embarrassment suggested more than professional collaboration. The way she'd caught herself, the flush in her cheeks when she mentioned his name—there was something personal there she wasn't ready to discuss.

"Fern, is there something else you're worried about? Something besides Dawn's questions?"

For a moment, I thought she might confide in me. She started to speak, then stopped. Her glance toward the main entrance suggested she was checking whether anyone might overhear.

"Sometimes things aren't what they first appear to be," she said quietly. Then, more firmly: "But some things aren't my secrets to tell."

That was the real source of her nervousness. Not just guilt about Dawn, but knowledge she was keeping to herself. Knowledge that involved someone else—someone she was protecting.

"I should get back," Fern said, checking her watch with obvious relief, grateful for an excuse to end the conversation. "The evening astronomy session starts soon."

"Of course. Thanks for showing me around."

As she collected her things, I studied her more carefully. Fern seemed genuinely naive about Dawn's manipulation, truly upset about her role in the memorial disruption. But she was definitely concealing something about personal relationships - the way she'd stopped herself from naming someone, the careful way she protected others' confidences.

Not exactly suspicious, but certainly incomplete. Like that 'K' rock—visible but unexplained, meaningful but mysterious.

And Dawn was revealing herself as far more calculating than the enthusiastic science communicator she appeared to be. Someone who'd systematically gathered intelligence about our community's private moments, who'd understood precisely how to present herself to extract needed information.

As footsteps echoed from the main entrance, I made my decision. Time to discover what Dawn had been researching -

and whether someone was helping her weaponize that research against my family.

As Fern collected her things and headed toward the exit, footsteps echoed from the main entrance, followed by familiar voices.

"...unusual properties when heated. Most people don't realize how distinctive the flame colour can be."

Sean's voice carried clearly through the museum's main hall, followed by the scrape of boxes being shifted and Charlie's low responses.

"That's fascinating. So different minerals actually change the colour of fire?"

"Absolutely. Copper compounds give you a vivid emerald green flame, sodium gives you yellow, lithium creates this brilliant red..." Sean's voice grew closer as they approached our section. "Fluorite's particularly interesting because it releases calcium fluoride when heated—creates this eerie blue-white flame, but you definitely don't want to breathe those fumes. Deadly toxic, actually."

I glanced at the mineral tray. Deadly. The word caught somewhere in my throat—strange thing to hear in a museum full of school projects and souvenir rocks.

Fern paused in the doorway, nodding to Sean and Charlie as they passed. "Good timing—I was just heading out for the evening astronomy session."

"Perfect," Sean said. "We'll get these specimens arranged for tomorrow's displays."

Charlie's smile was polite but brief. "Expecting a big crowd for your session tonight?"

"I hope so. The aurora forecast looks promising." Fern's enthusiasm was genuine as always.

"I'm sure it'll go well," Charlie said, though something in his tone suggested her growing popularity still rubbed him the wrong way.

As Fern left, I remained in the geology section with Des, who lifted her head from where she'd been resting near the display cases, ears pricked at the approaching voices.

Sean appeared carrying a wooden crate, with Charlie close behind balancing a stack of smaller boxes. Des padded over to sniff Charlie's boots before returning to my side with what could only be called a skeptical look.

"Afternoon, Tilly," Sean said, setting down his crate. "Just delivering the last of the specimens for the weekend displays."

Charlie carefully placed his boxes on a nearby table. "Sean's been explaining how different minerals behave when they burn. It's remarkable how varied the effects can be."

Sean began unpacking his crate, revealing several specimens wrapped in protective cloth. "Having someone handle the logistics while I focus on the technical side makes things more efficient." He paused, lifting out a wrapped specimen. "Though we're having some inventory issues—samples keep disappearing from the collection."

"Probably just misplaced in all the festival chaos," Charlie said helpfully.

"Maybe. But it's always the more interesting specimens that go missing." Sean shrugged and continued unpacking. "Lot of people helping out, things get moved around."

"I appreciate the opportunity to learn," Charlie said. "Why would someone want to know about burning minerals, anyway? Seems like dangerous knowledge."

Sean paused in his unpacking. "Academic curiosity, mostly.

Though some minerals have been misused throughout history. That's why proper handling is so important."

Des apparently had her own opinion about the afternoon's visitors—instead of her usual friendly interest in new people, she stayed pressed against my leg.

Her reaction was sharper than usual, though Des could be particular about some people.

The late afternoon light slanting through the tall windows cast long shadows across the polished floors, but the peaceful atmosphere felt at odds with the undercurrents I was sensing in this seemingly innocent work session.

Before I could dwell on it, rapid footsteps echoed from the main entrance.

"Mom!" Callie's voice carried urgent concern as she appeared in the doorway, phone clutched in her hand. "We need to talk. Now."

Sean and Charlie paused, sensing the tension.

"What's wrong?" I asked, immediately moving toward her.

Callie glanced at Sean and Charlie, then back at me. "Can we...?"

Sean checked his watch. "I'd better get back to the festival grounds—still have setup to finish before evening." He gathered his things efficiently, leaving Charlie to handle the remaining organization.

As Sean left, Charlie continued organizing the remaining specimens.

Once we had a bit of privacy, Callie showed me her phone. "It's turned into a full-on fight."

"Between who?"

"Everyone. Locals, outsiders—anyone with an opinion and Wi-Fi."

I took the phone, scrolling through the mess. The thread wasn't a discussion anymore; it was a shouting match typed in bold font. People defending Dawn. People defending us. Nobody listening.

"It's not about her anymore," I said quietly. "They're arguing about who we are."

Callie rubbed her forehead. "It's turning ugly, Mom."

"It already is."

"It gets more personal." Callie swiped to show me more comments. "Some of Dawn's followers are getting really aggressive about defending her methods."

"Mom, this isn't just random internet drama anymore," Callie's voice was tight with concern. "It's becoming locals versus outsiders, and it's getting nasty. People are taking sides over whether Dawn was right to film the memorial."

The implications hit me. The community was fracturing along the very lines Dawn had created.

"What about it?"

"I need to check something. Right now."

Charlie glanced up from his work, clearly having over-heard. "Everything alright?"

"Family matters," I said curtly, already moving toward the exit. "Come on, Des."

The walk to the house felt both urgent and surreal. Festival sounds drifted from the distance - music, laughter, the normal rhythms of community celebration. But my mind was racing through connections I should have made earlier.

We rushed through the house to Dad's study. Des trotted behind us, picking up on our urgency. The familiar room looked exactly as I'd left it.

I moved to Dad's desk and reached for the drawer handle, expecting the familiar resistance of the lock. Instead, the drawer slid open easily.

"Everything's gone," I whispered, staring at the empty space.

Callie peered over my shoulder. "What was in there?"

"Newspaper clippings, photocopies of old documents, some photos, I think—I hadn't gotten around to looking at them yet, handwritten notes about Samuel Melvin and the town's founding..." My voice trailed off as the full implication hit me. "Your grandfather was investigating something, but it wasn't clear what. Bertha must have put everything in the memorial box for the display."

"So whoever stole the box has all of Grandpa's research?"

"Someone needed that information badly enough to stage an elaborate disruption to steal it." I sank into Dad's chair, the weight of it all pressing down.

Callie sat on the edge of the desk. "The memorial wasn't the target—it was the cover."

"And Dawn was the perfect distraction. Someone had fed her just enough information to stir up maximum chaos at exactly the right moment."

"Mom, whoever has that box knows everything Grandpa discovered," Callie said, reading over my shoulder.

"Or they're looking for something specific." I watched Des continue to monitor the window, her alertness suggesting we might not be alone. "The question is whether they found what they wanted, or if they're still searching."

Des stiffened and padded to the window with a low whine. She pressed her nose to the glass, ears forward.

"What is it, girl?" I joined her at the window, scanning the street. Nothing obviously wrong, but Des's instincts were rarely mistaken.

Outside, the festival continued its cheerful celebration, unaware that someone in the community had orchestrated an elaborate theft of historical evidence. Someone who knew exactly what Dad had been investigating and why it needed to be silenced.

Someone still out there—watching, waiting to see if their plan had worked.

My phone buzzed. Jason: *Got some information. Meet me at the station tomorrow morning—8am.*

I showed Callie the text. "At least it's not urgent."

"Probably wants to coordinate before the festival gets crazy tomorrow," she said.

Des yawned, curling closer to the hearth. It had been a long day, and tomorrow promised to be longer.

CHAPTER EIGHT

Friday morning arrived too soon. I was heading to meet Jason when I spotted Sean and Arlo carrying boxes toward the museum. Des perked up, tugging the leash, nose twitching with interest.

Something about the tension in Arlo's shoulders made me pause. Jason could wait another few minutes.

"Morning," I called, following them into the museum. "Getting an early start?"

"Festival Day Three," Sean said. "Need to reset the displays after yesterday's crowds."

That's when I noticed his frown as he examined the cases. "This is getting ridiculous. More samples missing."

"Missing?" I moved closer.

"Several specimens have disappeared this week. Started Monday with some copper specimens, now a few of my good pieces are gone."

The morning light filtered through the tall windows, dust motes drifted across cases holding decades of town history. Arlo worked silently beside Sean, organizing sky-watching guides with unusual intensity.

"Which specimens exactly?" I asked, settling onto a nearby bench where Des immediately joined me.

"My best fluorite sample, some galena, a couple pieces of malachite." Sean's frustration was evident.

Arlo glanced up from his charts, something flickering across his expression. "Maybe it's just curious festival visitors taking souvenirs."

"These weren't on public display," Sean said. "They were in the storage room."

That caught my attention. Storage-room theft meant someone with access—someone who knew the layout as well as Fern did. "Who has keys to storage?"

"Fern, obviously. A few volunteers." Sean positioned a chunk of Manitoba agate where the light would catch its banding. "The coordination between all the displays has been working well, but now with pieces missing..."

"Speaking of missing things," I said. Deciding to be direct, I added, "I need to ask you about the memorial ceremony timing. You weren't there when it started."

Sean's hands stopped moving on the display case. Something shifted in his expression.

"No, I wasn't." Sean set down the specimen he'd been holding. "I should have been, but—"

"But what?"

He ran a hand through his hair. "I went straight from the church to the lake to make sure everything was set up for when people started arriving. But then I got a text from one of the festival volunteers saying there was an electrical emergency at the bandstand. They needed help right away."

"Can I see the text?" I asked.

Sean's brows lifted—not defensive, just taken aback. He

unlocked his phone anyway. I felt the small shift, a space opened between us—thin as glass, but sharp enough to feel.

He pulled out his phone, scrolled through, then handed it to me. The message was brief and urgent: *Electrical emergency bandstand URGENT - need help now. Sent at 7:43 PM.*

"That was exactly when the ceremony started," I said, handing back his phone.

"Just as it was starting. I tried to tell them it could wait, but they said it was a safety issue. Urgent." Sean's jaw tightened. "So I rushed over there. But when I got to the bandstand, there were only a couple volunteers around and they had no idea what I was talking about."

"No electrical problem?"

"Nothing. I called Charlotte to ask what was going on, but she didn't pick up. I checked everything myself—all the connections looked fine. By the time I gave up and headed back, everyone was already leaving. Bertha was there cleaning up with a few others." His voice got quieter. "That's when I found out what happened."

I watched his face while he talked. Sean wasn't hiding anything—if anything, he looked frustrated and a bit embarrassed. Someone had played him, pulled him away from the ceremony with a fake emergency.

"So you missed everything," I said.

"Completely. And I felt like an idiot afterward. If I'd been there, maybe I could've helped somehow." He picked up another specimen, turning it over in his hands. "Just frustrating to feel so manipulated, you know?"

"Someone wanted me specifically away from that memorial," Sean continued. "The timing was too perfect—they knew the memorial schedule down to the minute. Whoever did this knew exactly who could help and made sure we couldn't."

That hit me. Sean wasn't just offering sympathy—he

understood this was deliberate. His absence cleared him of involvement, but it also meant someone had thought through the details carefully enough to remove potential obstacles.

"This reminds me of corporate sabotage," Sean said, his professional side showing. "Remove key players, create chaos, achieve hidden objective. The memorial disruption was misdirection. The theft was the real goal."

"Any ideas who might've done it?" I asked.

Sean glanced toward the museum entrance, then back at me. "I've been thinking about it. But thinking and knowing are different things."

Before Sean could continue, Arlo shifted uncomfortably, his voice tight. "You keep acting like Dawn's just some innocent podcaster. She's not."

I turned to look at him. "What do you mean?"

"I mean she's..." Arlo's hands clenched the guides in front of him, his face flushing. "She's not here just for the festival. She's got her own agenda."

"What kind of agenda?"

His defensiveness flared. "The kind where she digs into people's personal business. Makes everything about drama instead of science."

"Arlo, do you know Dawn from somewhere?"

"We've crossed paths." The admission came reluctantly. "Conference circuit. She did a piece on aurora predictions that made me look incompetent."

Sean watched this exchange with growing interest.

"So when she showed up here..." I began.

"When she showed up here, she recognized me immediately." Arlo's voice got sharper. "Started asking questions about..." He looked annoyed, running a hand through his hair. "Personal stuff that's nobody's business."

"And you told her to back off?"

"Of course I did. But she doesn't listen." He threw down the guides. "Look, some people use science as a way to exploit others, and Dawn's one of them. That's all I'm saying."

He headed for the door, clearly wanting to escape the conversation. "You want to trust her? Fine. But don't say I didn't warn you."

He stormed out, leaving Sean and me staring after him.

"Well," Sean said quietly with a slight smirk, "that was illuminating."

Before I could respond, my phone rang. Jason's name appeared on the screen, and I realized I'd kept him waiting.

"Tilly, where are you? I've been waiting at the station." His voice carried irritation that quickly shifted to urgency. "Never mind that now. We found the memorial box."

My heart jumped. "Where?"

"Dumped behind the community centre. But Tilly..." He paused. "Most of the contents are missing. Just some trinkets left behind. Whoever took it got what they wanted and ditched the rest."

I sank onto the bench, the disappointment hitting like a physical blow. "So the evidence is gone."

"Looks that way. The box was ransacked, not just stolen. They knew exactly what to take and what to leave."

Maybe Dad found something he wasn't supposed to—old mining secrets, things the Bugles wouldn't want anyone digging up. The thought came unbidden, sharp as the cold air.

After I hung up, Sean studied my expression. "Bad news?"

"The memorial box turned up, but it's been gutted. They took what they wanted and left the rest behind." I stood up, feeling the weight of the setback. "The trail's going cold."

Des pressed against my leg, offering comfort.

Sean's expression tightened. "I'm sorry, Tilly. That's awful. After everything your family's been through..."

"Thanks," I said, my voice tired. "I should probably get going. Jason's waiting."

I hesitated. "Sean, if you notice anything else—anything that feels off—will you let me know?"

"Of course." His answer came without hesitation. "We're on the same side here, Tilly. Whatever else is complicated between us, that's not."

The words landed gently enough, but they stung all the same. Maybe because I wanted to believe him. Maybe because I already did.

Walking out of the museum with Des, I felt the investigation slipping away from me.

Sean had his secrets, but he'd been straightforward about missing the ceremony, and he had his own problems with specimens going missing. Arlo's defensive reaction about Dawn suggested more history than he'd admitted. Now the memorial box had been found stripped of anything useful.

Whoever was behind this stayed one step ahead—covering tracks, erasing proof. The urgency I'd felt walking in had only intensified.

It wasn't whether I could solve this anymore—it was whether I could do it before they struck again.

After the phone call with Jason, I needed to keep moving. Sitting still would only let the frustration build—and I'd promised to help with the festival preparations anyway.

Des and I walked into the community centre's organized chaos.

Long tables stretched across the main room, covered with an impressive array of festival gift bags, each one carefully labeled with campsite numbers. Volunteers worked with determined efficiency, sorting, stuffing, and tying ribbons at stations throughout the busy space.

"Tilly!" Kelli called from behind a mountain of printed festival programs. "Perfect timing. We could use another pair of hands."

I surveyed the scene with Des at my side. Clusters of residents worked at different stations—some folding maps and information sheets, others organizing pre-made packets and vouchers, and still others assembling finished bags into distribution boxes that Charlie moved between stations with practiced efficiency.

Near the far end of the room, Fern and Arlo were working together at one of the supply tables, their heads bent over a stack of labeled boxes. Fern appeared absorbed in sorting the star charts, while Arlo checked lists against his phone, keeping the pace brisk. They didn't notice us come in—just two more volunteers in the organized chaos of the hall.

"This is quite the operation," I said, approaching Kelli's station. "How many bags are you preparing?"

"A few hundred," said Mabel, looking up from a pile of festival pins. "Vendors get one as a thank you gift, Charlotte's VIPs each get one, one goes to every registered campsite, and we'll have some extras to give away as we see fit."

"Each bag has festival information, one of Fern's star charts, a campfire colour packet, some of my aurora tea blend, plus vouchers for local businesses," Kelli explained, holding up a completed bag. "Took weeks to coordinate, but everyone should get a nice taste of what Balsam Bay has to offer."

I picked up one of the small packets labeled "Aurora Fire." The powder inside shifted like ground gemstones. "What are these?"

"Sean's idea, actually," Kelli said. "The kids will love it! Some kind of mineral powder that changes flame colours when you toss it in a campfire. He thought it would add to the whole aurora theme. Haven't you seen them before? My dad used to get these for us when we went camping."

"No, I haven't. Clever," I said, watching Charlie appear at another table with perfect timing, coordinating the final assembly with almost suspicious efficiency. Des stayed close to my side, more alert than usual.

Charlie reappeared with another box. "How are we doing with the tea samples?" he asked, setting it down carefully. "I want to make sure each bag has the right materials."

"All sorted," Mabel said. "Though you really know your way around this operation."

"Just trying to be helpful," Charlie said with that easy smile. "Charlotte's got high standards for the festival experience."

"He's been everywhere today," I noted, trying to keep my tone casual.

"Charlotte's got him running volunteer coordination," Mabel said approvingly. "Boy's got a real talent for keeping things running."

"He's really got this organized," I said, watching Charlie help an elderly volunteer reach items on a high shelf.

"Oh, he's not putting on airs about it either," Kelli added. "Yesterday he spent an hour helping Mrs. Henderson sort out her part of the packing list. Could've done it himself in ten minutes, but he made sure she understood the whole process."

As Charlie moved to help at another station, I noticed Des tracking his movement with unusual intensity.

"He's been such a help," Kelli murmured. "Charlotte really lucked out with that one."

"Speaking of help," I said, settling into a rhythm with the gift bag assembly, "how has Dawn been settling in? I know she's been talking to people around town."

The change in Kelli's expression was immediate. "Well," she said slowly, "she did stop by my shop yesterday. Asked quite a few questions."

"What kind of questions?"

"About local families, community history. Your family specifically." Kelli's voice dropped. "Asked about your investigation experience, Tilly. Very detailed questions."

That caught my attention. "Detailed how?"

"She wanted to know about your search and rescue background, how long you'd been doing that kind of work. Asked whether you'd ever had cases that didn't work out the way you'd hoped." Kelli frowned. "Almost like she was looking for pressure points."

The phrase sent a chill through me. "Pressure points?" I repeated.

"That's what it felt like," Mabel added, joining the conversation. "She seemed to know quite a bit already about what happened this summer. Asked very specific questions about how you'd handled things, whether the community trusted your judgment."

I felt something cold settle in my stomach. "What else did she want to know?"

"She asked about the memorial planning," Kelli continued. "Wanted to know who was involved, how decisions got made, even details about the timing."

"The timing?"

"When things were scheduled, how people knew what to do when. Almost like she was trying to understand how community events get organized." Kelli's voice dropped further. "Which seems like odd research for someone who was supposedly surprised by what happened."

"Did she ask about other people too?"

"The festival committee mostly. Charlotte's family background, how long people had lived here. Even asked about Sean." Mabel paused in her sorting. "At the time I thought she was just being thorough, but thinking back..."

"It felt more like she was looking for something specific," Kelli finished.

I glanced around the busy hall. Charlie was organizing different distribution areas now, moving with practiced efficiency.

"The thing that bothered me most," Kelli continued, "was how systematic she was. Had this notebook and kept writing things down. Even recorded our whole conversation."

"She recorded you without asking?"

"Claimed it was for ambient sound for her podcast, but she had it running even during personal conversation." Mabel's disapproval was clear. "Made me uncomfortable afterward."

The picture was getting clearer and uglier. Dawn hadn't been gathering information casually—she'd been systematically documenting conversations, noting every weakness in how our community worked.

"You know what's interesting?" I said, thinking out loud. "Did she ask about Charlie specifically?"

Kelli and Mabel exchanged glances.

"No," Kelli said slowly. "I can't recall that she did."

"She asked about Charlotte, Sean, the festival committee, my family. But not Charlie." I watched him coordinate with volunteers across the room. "Maybe she didn't see him as relevant to whatever story she was planning."

Before anyone could respond, hurried footsteps announced Callie's arrival. She burst through the hall doors, laptop bag slung over her shoulder and worry etched across her face.

"Mom, it's bad."

"Define bad."

She opened her screen. The glow hit me like floodlight—

rows of comments spilling faster than she could scroll. Angry faces, half-truths, locals snapping at strangers.

Around us, volunteers' phones buzzed in unison. You didn't need to read the thread to feel the temperature rising.

"They're calling us secretive. Corrupt."

I swallowed hard. "They don't even know us."

"They don't need to—they've already found a story they like better."

"It gets worse." Callie scrolled further, the screen filling with more comments. "Dawn's fans are defending her methods really aggressively. They're saying journalism should make people uncomfortable—that exposure matters more than privacy."

"Mom, this is exactly what I was afraid of." Callie's voice tightened with worry. "It's becoming us versus them. The community is splitting into those who think Dawn was justified and those who think she crossed a line."

I looked around the hall full of volunteers preparing welcome gifts for visitors. The contrast between their genuine care and this online battleground felt stark.

"You need to moderate more heavily," I said.

"I know. But if I delete the criticism of Dawn, people will say I'm censoring. If I delete the defence of her, they'll say I'm biased against journalism." Callie's journalistic instincts were at war with her protective feelings. "I'm caught in the middle, Mom."

Des pressed against my leg, picking up the shift in tension.

"The worst part is some of Dawn's followers are getting really nasty about our family specifically," Callie continued. "Saying we're trying to hide something, that we don't want the truth to come out."

The pieces clicked together with horrible clarity. Dawn's systematic research. Her detailed questions about community dynamics and vulnerabilities. Her perfect timing at the memorial. Now her supporters were using the blog to attack anyone who questioned her methods.

"Dawn's been feeding information to her followers," I said —the certainty hit me like a physical blow. "She came here planning to create drama, not document it."

"What are you going to do?" Callie asked.

"Confront her. Tonight, before whatever she has planned can happen." I stood up, decision crystallizing. "She's been using our community's openness against us, but that ends now."

Charlie appeared at our table with perfect timing. "Everything alright? You both look upset."

"Just some blog drama," I said carefully. "People getting heated about journalism ethics."

"Well, if you need any help coordinating things, just let me know," Charlie offered with apparent sincerity. "I know how these online situations can get complicated."

Des positioned herself between Charlie and me, a low rumble in her throat.

"Thanks, but we've got it covered," I said, noting how Des was reacting to his proximity.

As Charlie moved away, I felt the weight of the evening ahead. Dawn had systematically gathered information about our community, used it to create maximum drama, and now her supporters were using that chaos to attack anyone who questioned her methods.

"Dawn thinks she's been clever," I told Callie quietly. "But she doesn't understand that communities protect their own."

The festival preparations continued around us, volunteers working with cheerful efficiency. But underneath the surface, I could feel the community fracturing along the lines Dawn had deliberately created - those who believed in her right to docu-

ment everything versus those who felt she'd violated something sacred.

Des stayed pressed against my leg as we prepared to leave, her instincts clearly telling her that tension was building. The Aurora Fire might be beautiful tonight, but something told me they'd illuminate more than just the campfire.

CHAPTER NINE

A few hours after the gift-bag assembly, the bustle of the community centre had faded into the quieter rhythm of the store. Callie and I had been back at the store since mid-afternoon, working through orders while she kept one eye on her blog. By closing time, her earlier anxiety had settled into focused determination. She'd spent the last few hours moderating carefully—deleting the worst trolling while preserving legitimate discussion. The stress of managing her platform responsibly showed in the tight set of her shoulders.

"I need to lock up the till," I said, watching her close the laptop with deliberate care.

Des stretched beside the counter, recognizing the evening routine. The store felt different after hours—quieter, more like the place Dad had built than the tourist destination it had become during festival week.

My phone buzzed with a text from Mandy: *Sean, Bertha, and I heading up to Aurora Point around 8:30. Arlo says tonight's conditions are perfect. You two should come! The Belles are organizing a group from the community centre.*

"Mandy's going up to Aurora Point tonight," I told Callie, showing her the message. "Want to join them?"

"Absolutely." Callie's face brightened for the first time all day. "I could use some perspective that isn't screen-sized."

Aurora Point meant a proper hike, even with the maintained trail. We gathered warm layers and headlamps, then drove to the trailhead, where a cheerful volunteer with a clipboard checked off names.

"Perfect timing," she said, checking our names off. "There's a lovely group already up there, and the aurora forecast is exceptional."

The trail wound through dense forest, marked by reflective tags that caught our flashlight beams. Des trotted ahead with tail-wagging enthusiasm, her white patches visible in the darkness as she investigated scents and sounds that held no interest for humans.

After twenty minutes of steady climbing, the trees opened up, and Aurora Point spread before us—a wide, flat expanse of granite jutting out over Echo Lake like nature's own observation deck.

The view from Aurora Point was breathtaking, even in darkness. Echo Lake stretched out below us, its black surface reflecting the scattered lights of Balsam Bay like fallen stars. The elevated position made everything feel both intimate and infinite—close enough to see individual cabin windows, distant enough to appreciate the wilderness that surrounded our small community.

Mandy waved us over to where she, Sean, and Bertha had claimed a spot near the centre of the granite platform. The Belles had taken over the eastern edge, their chairs aligned with the precision of a quilting pattern. Nora had brought what appeared to be a vintage thermos, while Enid consulted a laminated star chart with a small red flashlight.

"Right on time," Mandy called softly. "Arlo says the Kp index hit 4 this afternoon and the solar wind is picking up speed." She paused and grinned. "I won't pretend to know what that means, but all I need to know is there's supposed to be a good light show tonight."

About thirty people had gathered on Aurora Point, a mix of locals and festival visitors who'd secured spots through the rotation system. Families spread blankets on the smooth granite while photographers set up tripods with quiet efficiency. The atmosphere was expectant but peaceful—people who understood instinctively that this was a place for whispers and wonder.

Enid leaned forward from her lawn chair, lowering her voice as if sharing something precious. "You know, Aurora Point wasn't named for the northern lights at all."

Nora looked up from her star chart. "Oh, here we go."

"It's true!" Enid insisted. "The story's older than Balsam Bay itself. Roman goddess Aurora, bringer of the dawn. She travelled east to west every morning, waking the world as she went."

Nora jumped in before Enid could build too much momentum. "And she stopped right here—halfway across her journey. Paused at Balsam Bay before carrying on west."

"People follow all kinds of paths here, chasing something," Enid continued, warming to her theme. "Some stay, become part of the place." She glanced meaningfully at me. "Others just pass through, taking what they need before moving on."

"Or maybe," Nora said dryly, "she was just tired of dragging the sun around. Can't blame her for wanting a rest."

Enid sniffed but pressed on. "The point is, this was always a place of pausing. Of choosing. That podcaster, now—she came from the east, too, chasing the lights. But Aurora brought more than just the dawn—she brought the sun itself across the sky. And those who get too close to what they're chasing..." Enid's voice trailed off meaningfully. "Well, sometimes the lights that promise wonder can burn."

The weight of her words settled over our little group, made heavier by the dancing lights overhead.

Des immediately began exploring the perimeter of the platform, nose working overtime on the fascinating scents left by wildlife that used this rocky outcrop. Her tail wagged as she investigated every crevice and boulder, but she kept a respectful distance from the edge.

The first hints of aurora appeared as faint green wisps along the northern horizon, so subtle they could have been mistaken for clouds. But gradually, unmistakably, they began to move with their own rhythm. The colours strengthened and spread, painting the sky in shades of green that had no earthly equivalent.

"There," Sean said quietly, pointing to where the lights were beginning to dance more boldly. "It's starting."

The gathered crowd fell into that hushed reverence that comes from witnessing something genuinely magical. Adults and children alike tilted their heads back, watching the sky transform into something out of a dream. Even seasoned locals like Bertha seemed transfixed by the display.

Aurora Point's elevation made the lights feel close enough to touch. The granite platform provided perfect viewing angles in every direction, and the lack of light pollution made colours visible that would be lost in town. Green ribbons folded over themselves, occasionally shot through with hints of purple and blue that made people gasp.

"This is why we protect this place," Bertha said quietly, her voice carrying the weight of someone who'd fought those battles personally. "Not just the rock, but what happens when people connect with something bigger than themselves."

The cool October air carried a mix of fallen leaves and distant chimney smoke, the scent of early winter creeping in. Night birds called from the forest, their voices mixing with the gentle sound of small waves against the cliff base. A loon's haunting call echoed across the water, answered by another from somewhere deeper in the wilderness.

Mandy's hot chocolate was perfect—rich and warming, with just a hint of cinnamon that cut through the evening chill. She'd brought enough for everyone nearby, passing around paper cups with the kind of generous spirit that made communities work.

"You're carrying everyone's burdens again," Mandy said quietly, settling beside me as we watched Callie document the aurora's dance. "When's the last time you just let yourself be present for something beautiful?"

She was right. The stress of the investigation didn't disappear, but it receded enough to let me appreciate this moment —the community gathering, the natural beauty, the genuine connections happening all around us under dancing lights.

Callie moved carefully through the crowd, capturing photographs that would help her blog followers understand why people travelled thousands of miles for this experience. But she was doing it thoughtfully, never using flash, never disrupting the natural rhythm of wonder that had settled over Aurora Point.

"The colours are getting stronger," Sean observed, looking up at the sky where green had given way to brilliant dancing curtains. "This could be one of the best displays of the season."

Loud voices rose from the trail below, growing closer with each passing minute. Heavy footsteps and the clatter of equipment cut through the whispered conversations and reverent silence that had naturally developed among the aurora watchers.

"This way, everyone! Premium viewing experience begins now!" Charlotte's voice carried clearly through the crisp air, her tone pitched for maximum impact.

A group of about fifteen tourists emerged from the tree line, led by Charlotte with the kind of aggressive energy that suggested schedules to keep and experiences to deliver. They moved with the slightly frantic urgency of people who'd paid extra for exclusivity and intended to get their money's worth.

Dawn followed behind them, camera equipment at the ready, documenting everything with the methodical approach I'd observed throughout the festival. She was interviewing tourists as they climbed, asking leading questions while the lights danced overhead, utterly indifferent to her schedule.

"What are you hoping to see in tonight's aurora display?" Dawn asked one of the tourists, her recorder positioned to capture both response and ambient sound.

"Exclusive Premium Viewing Experience," Charlotte butted in, seemingly oblivious to the thirty people who'd been peacefully enjoying Aurora Point for the past hour. "Away from the regular crowds, with expert guidance about optimal photography angles and aurora science."

Charlotte's group had come prepared for luxury. Branded lanterns lit their way, sturdy lawn chairs were quickly positioned as close to the cliff edge as safety allowed, and a portable table appeared with wine and light snacks. Two people I didn't recognize began setting up telescopes with professional efficiency.

The new arrivals immediately claimed the choicest viewing spots, talking loudly about camera settings and exposure times while children who'd been quietly marvelling at the lights suddenly found themselves pushed back from the granite platform's edge.

"Excuse me," one of Charlotte's tourists said to Bertha,

who was sitting peacefully in her folding chair. "Could you move? You're blocking our view of the lake reflection."

Bertha's expression could have frozen the aurora itself. She didn't move.

Dawn continued her methodical documentation, filming the gathered crowd and treating the evening like a performance staged for tourist entertainment. When a young boy pointed excitedly at a particularly bright green spiral, Dawn immediately positioned herself to capture his reaction, transforming his genuine wonder into content.

"She's documenting us like specimens," I murmured to Callie, watching Dawn work with calculating efficiency.

Charlotte bragged loudly about her "insider access" and "curated experience," while Dawn gathered quotes about the "authentic community experience" her tourists were witnessing. The two women worked in perfect coordination—Charlotte providing exclusive access while Dawn crafted the narrative that would attract more premium customers.

Dawn caught me watching. She looked directly at me across the granite platform, smiled, and gave a small wave with her camera—a gesture that felt like both acknowledgment and challenge.

The casual arrogance of it crystallized everything I'd suspected. Dawn wasn't just documenting our community— she was orchestrating something. And she wanted me to know it.

At home, I couldn't stop thinking about Dawn's calculating smile.

"Mom, you need to see this," Callie said, settling at the kitchen table with her laptop. "The comment section is exploding. Dawn's followers versus the locals, and it's getting really ugly."

I leaned over Callie's shoulder. Her feed was a flood—comments multiplying faster than she could moderate.

"Every time I delete one, three more appear," she said.

"That's coordinated," I murmured. "Someone's feeding this."

The words hit the air heavier than I meant them to; coordinated meant planned. Planned meant deliberate.

"She's weaponizing her platform against our community," I said, watching the criticism pile up in real time. "Her followers are attacking anyone who questions her methods."

"But why?" Callie asked, looking up from the screen. "What does she get out of targeting us specifically?"

The question stopped me short. Dawn was a travel blogger with thousands of followers—why would she focus so intensely on our small family crisis? "Content," I said finally. "Drama gets clicks. Our pain is profitable for her."

"What are you going to do?"

"I'm going over there," I said, already standing. "I can't just sit here while she does this to us."

Des immediately rose from her spot beside the fireplace, sensing the shift in my energy. Her ears pricked forward, alert to whatever had changed my mood from frustrated to determined.

I grabbed my jacket and headed for the door, Des at my side.

Walking past downtown, I could see the festival information booths had closed for the night, their cheerful banners hanging limp in the still air. A few of Charlotte's VIP group members were making their way back from the Aurora Point trailhead, chatting quietly about their exclusive experience as they headed toward their accommodations.

The campground had settled into evening rhythms. Most campsites glowed with evening fires and the quiet sounds of families settling in for the night.

Dawn's trailer sat at the far edge of the camping area, lights on and clearly occupied. As we approached, I could see Dawn outside organizing her camera equipment, probably reviewing footage from the evening's coverage.

Perfect. A private conversation was exactly what this situation required.

Des trotted ahead, drawn by the interesting scents near Dawn's setup, but stayed close when I approached the trailer area.

"Working late?" I asked, stepping into the circle of light from Dawn's setup.

Dawn looked up and smiled with professional brightness. "Tilly! Didn't expect to see you again tonight. Just organizing gear for tomorrow. What brings you by?"

"I know what you did at the memorial," I said. "Someone told you exactly when and where to show up. You didn't just stumble into that—someone set you up to disrupt it."

Dawn's smile faded. "Set me up? Tilly, I was the one who got set up. Someone told me it was a public festival event."

"And you're protecting whoever told you that."

"Because I'm trying to figure out why," Dawn said, getting frustrated. "Someone used me to hurt your family. Don't you want to know who?"

"You're the one who showed up with cameras."

"I thought I was documenting a community celebration!" Dawn's composure slipped. "Someone gave me completely wrong information. That's not journalism—that's manipulation."

"Then tell me who," I said. "If you were really manipulated, prove it."

Dawn set down whatever she'd been fiddling with. "I protect my sources, even when they lie to me."

"That's going to be a problem when Jason questions you tomorrow," I said. "Refusing to identify who helped you stage what became a crime scene makes you an accessory."

Dawn's expression shifted. "I didn't help steal anything."

"Tell that to the RCMP. Either you were duped or you were involved. Either way, you'll have to give up your source or face obstruction charges."

"I'm trying to protect you."

"Protect me?" I couldn't help the skepticism in my voice. "By turning my family's grief into content?"

"By finding out who's really behind this," Dawn said. "You think I wanted to ruin your memorial? I've felt sick about it since it happened. But someone planned that whole thing."

Her conviction gave me pause, but only for a second. "Convenient story. Blame some mystery person while you profit from the mess."

"There's something bigger going on here," Dawn said. "The timing, how precise the information was—someone wanted to hurt your family badly. Don't you want to know who?"

"I'm looking at her."

Dawn laughed, but there was no humour in it. "You're looking at the weapon, not the person who aimed it. Someone used me to hurt you."

"Then help me understand," I said, running out of patience. "Stop hiding behind journalism if you really want to help."

"I can't reveal sources while I'm still investigating," Dawn said. "But I'm getting close. Someone in this community wanted your memorial disrupted."

The way she talked about our pain like a puzzle to solve made my skin crawl.

"Whatever your excuses," I said, "you turned our private moment into entertainment."

"I documented what happened because someone made it happen," Dawn said. "And until I figure out who and why, your family could still be in danger."

"Is that a threat?"

"It's a warning," Dawn said quietly. "Someone used me once. They could use someone else."

Des moved closer to my side, picking up on the tension crackling between us. Her presence grounded me just enough to keep from saying something I might actually regret.

"We're done here," I said, turning to leave.

"For what it's worth," Dawn called after me, "I am sorry people got hurt. But I'm going to find out who's really responsible for this."

I didn't look back. Her defensive explanations, her claims about being manipulated, her refusal to name sources—everything about our conversation had confirmed that she was hiding something important.

I was still processing Dawn's justifications when I heard familiar footsteps approaching across the gravel. Des perked up, tail wagging at the sound of someone she recognized.

"Tilly!" Fern's voice was bright and cheerful as she emerged from between two campsites, a canvas tote bag in her hands and a bright pink toque perched on her head despite the mild evening. The hat was the kind of vibrant colour that stood out even in dim light, clearly hand-knitted with slightly irregular stitches that suggested it had been made with love rather than professional precision.

"How are you holding up with all this festival excitement?" she asked.

"Fine," I said, though my voice probably betrayed some of the anger I was still feeling. "Just making the rounds."

"Same here," Fern said with a laugh, lifting the tote bag. "One more delivery to go, then I can finally relax and enjoy the evening. These gift bags are heavier than they look when you're carrying dozens of them."

Dawn had emerged from her trailer again, clearly having overheard our conversation.

"Fern!" Dawn said with genuine warmth. "Perfect timing. How did the rest of your deliveries go?"

"Almost done," Fern said cheerfully, extending the labeled tote toward Dawn. "Festival gift bag delivery—I saved yours for last since you're our special guest."

Dawn accepted the bag with obvious pleasure, immediately peering inside at the contents. "This is so thoughtful. What's all this?"

"Festival information, local business vouchers, some of Kelli's special aurora tea blend," Fern listed off enthusiastically. "There's also a pin, a map of the best aurora viewing spots, a voucher for Mandy's bakery, and one of those campfire colour packets."

"Colour packet?" Dawn's professional interest was clearly piqued.

"Powders that change the colour of campfire flames," Fern explained. "Thought it would add to the whole aurora theme. Might be worth getting a photo or two when people use them."

Dawn was already reaching for her camera. "That sounds like great footage."

"I was hoping you'd say that!" Fern's smile was radiant. "It would be wonderful to have it documented properly."

Then Fern winced slightly, pressing one hand to her lower back. "Oh, this camping adventure is harder than I expected. I thought staying in a tent would be fun—you know, the full festival experience—but my back's killing me. I'm really not looking forward to another night on the ground."

"You're camping in a tent?" Dawn asked. "That's real dedication to the festival spirit."

"Well, I wanted to experience what our visitors do," Fern said with a rueful laugh. "But I'm really not cut out for camping. I had no idea how uncomfortable sleeping on the ground would be."

"You know," Dawn said thoughtfully, "I feel terrible that you're suffering for the festival with all that you're doing. Why don't you take my trailer tonight? I actually love sleeping under the stars—it's perfect for aurora watching. And I'll use your tent, if that's okay with you."

"Oh, I couldn't possibly—" Fern began, but her relief was obvious.

"Really, I insist," Dawn said. "You've been so welcoming since I arrived. It's the least I can do."

As I walked away with Des, watching Fern hurry toward her campsite to gather her things, my mind was churning over every word of my confrontation with Dawn.

Her defensive explanations, her protection of sources, her claims about being used—everything about our conversation had left me more convinced that she was involved in orchestrating the memorial disruption.

"She basically admitted someone fed her information," I told Callie when we reached the main festival area. "But she's protecting them while her followers attack our community online. That makes her complicit."

"What are you going to do?" Callie asked.

"Talk to Jason tomorrow. Dawn isn't just an outside observer who stumbled into controversy—she's actively protecting whoever targeted my family while using her platform to defend exploitation as journalism."

Whether she was the mastermind or just a willing accomplice, Dawn was hiding the truth about who had hurt us. Her refusal to cooperate while continuing to profit from our pain and turning her followers loose on anyone who questioned her methods made her just as guilty as whoever had fed her the information.

I knew exactly what I was dealing with now.

CHAPTER TEN

I left Dawn's trailer with Des at my side, the confrontation still churning through my mind. The festival grounds stretched ahead of us, golden with the warm glow of paper lanterns strung between camping spots—but my thoughts were locked on Dawn's defensive responses and evasive answers.

"She's protecting someone," I muttered to Des, who looked up at me with those intelligent brown eyes. "People don't get that evasive unless they're hiding something significant."

Des pressed closer to my leg, picking up on my agitation. Her easy trot shifted into something more alert, protective.

"Let's take a walk, girl. I need to clear my head."

The evening air was crisp but pleasant, carrying a faint trace of wood smoke. We headed through the campground toward home, past the organized rows of tents and trailers where families were settling in for the night.

Multiple campsites glowed with the warm light of campfires, and I could hear children's excited voices mixed with their parents' laughter. The Aurora Fire packets were clearly being put to good use—purple and green and brilliant orange flames danced above the logs as families took turns tossing their mineral powders into the fires.

The sight was beautiful, actually. Sean's idea had worked perfectly, transforming ordinary campfires into something magical as the coloured flames painted wonder on children's faces. Parents scrambled to capture photos and videos, cameras clicking as each new packet transformed the flames into a fresh spectacle.

At one campsite, a little girl squealed with delight as her packet turned the flames a brilliant emerald green. At another, twin boys argued over whose turn it was next while their father refereed with good-natured patience.

The peaceful scene stood in sharp contrast to the turmoil in my thoughts. Here was the festival at its best—families creating memories, community traditions bringing people together, the simple joy of shared wonder. Everything Dawn claimed to document, but somehow made complicated with her questions and implications.

We passed Fern's assigned campsite, where Dawn sat alone by her fire, examining the contents of a gift bag. She took out one of the campfire colour packets, turning it over in her hands before tossing it into the flames with idle curiosity.

Des shifted restlessly beside me, her nose working the air before she nudged closer to my leg.

"Tomorrow, Jason deals with her," I told Des, feeling some of the tension leave my shoulders. Whatever game Dawn was playing, whatever information she was hiding, I'd done what I could. The official investigation would have to take it from here.

We continued past more campsites where the evening was winding down. Other families were banking their fires and settling children into sleeping bags, the excited whispers and giggles gradually giving way to the deeper quiet of a community preparing for sleep.

Des stayed alert to the night sounds—the rustle of canvas, the soft murmur of late conversations, the distant call of a loon from the lake. Her ears swivelled at every noise, but she remained calm and focused.

By now, the main festival area was quiet; the organized activities had wrapped up hours earlier. We were at the halfway point of the festival, and it was winding down successfully despite everything that had happened over the past few days.

Exhausted but relieved, I felt certain I'd identified the problem. Dawn might not be the mastermind, but she was definitely hiding crucial information about who had manipulated her into disrupting Dad's memorial. Her refusal to cooperate—while profiting from our pain—made her complicit, whatever her role.

As we neared the edge of the campground, Des froze, muscles taut, ears pricked forward. I followed her gaze and saw a figure walking past us with nervous, purposeful strides, heading back toward the campsites.

Arlo, moving through the shadows with obvious intention. Even in the dim light, I recognized his lanky frame and distinctive gait. But there was something different about his posture—tense and furtive in a way that sparked my curiosity.

"What's he up to?" I whispered. Des stayed perfectly still, her instincts razor-sharp.

Instinct overrode propriety. I pulled Des behind a cluster of recycling bins and watched as Arlo moved purposefully along the gravel lane.

He moved with purpose through the quiet campground, heading toward the lakeview sites. When he reached Dawn's trailer and knocked softly on the door—a careful, measured sound that suggested he was trying not to wake nearby campers—I held my breath.

It opened, revealing Fern in the doorway, backlit by the trailer's warm interior light. Arlo's reaction made me lean forward. He actually stepped back, surprise flashing across his face. This was clearly not who he'd expected to find.

Even from a distance, I could see the confusion on Fern's face shift rapidly to something sharper. Her posture went rigid as she took in Arlo's presence there, this late at night.

Arlo pushed his glasses up his nose as he recovered, his hands coming up in what looked like a placating gesture, his voice carrying the urgent cadence of someone trying to explain themselves. But Fern's body language told the real story—arms crossed defensively, her stance suggesting she was both hurt and angry.

That wasn't the reaction of a casual acquaintance—it was personal, the hurt look of someone who'd just uncovered a truth she wished she hadn't.

The exchange lasted barely three minutes—long enough for my mind to spin through every troubling possibility. When Fern finally stepped back and closed the trailer door, Arlo stood there for several long moments before turning away, his shoulders sagging with what looked like defeat.

As he turned back toward the main campground, light from a nearby lantern caught his face. Worried. Frustrated. And something else—something that looked almost like fear. But anger, too, simmering beneath the surface.

Des hadn't moved the whole time—tense, alert. Now she looked up at me, questioning, as if to ask what we'd just witnessed.

"I don't know," I whispered back. "But that definitely wasn't about aurora forecasts."

Whatever was happening between Arlo and Fern, it was

connected to something larger than festival logistics. The timing—late at night, when most people were asleep, when private conversations could happen without community oversight—suggested it was something they didn't want others to know about.

But I was too tired to analyze it properly tonight. Too emotionally drained from the confrontation with Dawn, too frustrated by all the secrets and evasions that seemed to surround this festival.

As we finally made our way home, Des staying close to my side as if sensing my unease, I found myself questioning everything I thought I knew about the people involved in this situation.

Dawn might be hiding something, but she wasn't the only one with secrets. If Arlo and Fern had their own complicated history, their own reasons for private midnight conversations, then maybe the web of relationships here was more tangled than I'd realized.

Maybe my focus on Dawn—the obvious outsider—had blinded me to the undercurrents already swirling within our own community.

Friday morning arrived too soon, heralded by Des's insistent whining at my bedroom door. I'd finally fallen asleep sometime after two, my dreams fragmented—snatches of midnight conversations and hidden agendas. The interaction between Arlo and Fern kept replaying in my mind—his shock at finding her in the trailer, her obvious hurt and anger, the way their entire exchange had felt heavy with unspoken history.

Sunlight streamed through the curtains—autumn-gold

and slanted—promising a perfect morning for the festival's third day. Des was making it clear she needed to go outside.

"Alright, alright," I muttered, pulling on yesterday's clothes and grabbing her leash. My jeans were rumpled, the sweater still faintly scented of last night's wood smoke. "But this is just a quick trip to the yard, and then we're coming back for proper coffee."

Des had other ideas. The moment we stepped outside, she lunged toward the festival grounds with the kind of determination that suggested something had caught her attention. Her nose was working overtime, testing the morning air for scents that apparently required immediate investigation. This wasn't her usual leisurely morning sniffing routine—this was focused, urgent.

"Come on, Des. Just do your business so we can go back inside."

But she was already tugging me down the path toward the campground, her entire body focused on something I couldn't detect. I'd learned to trust her instincts this summer—both during the mystery surrounding Dad's disappearance and in the weeks since. My SAR K9 experience had taught me the hard way what happened when you ignored a dog's alerts. When Des insisted on investigating something, there was usually a good reason.

The campground was still mostly quiet in that peaceful way of early morning, though a few early risers were moving around their campsites. I could see someone starting a camp stove near the far edge of the grounds, the blue flame flickering in the morning air. Another camper was hanging wet towels on a line strung between two trees, the domestic routines of people making the most of their outdoor adventure.

Wood smoke lingered from last night's fires, mingling with crisp air and dew-damp grass. But underneath those familiar camping smells was something else—something that made Des's ears flatten against her gait turned cautious.

I found myself cataloguing details as we walked, a habit that kicked in whenever something felt off. The way the morning light filtered through the trees, casting long shadows between the campsites. The sound of someone running water at a hand-washing station. The distant murmur of voices from early risers planning their day.

Everything looked normal—peaceful, even. Families were slowly emerging from tents and trailers, children's voices mixing with the gentle sounds of breakfast preparation. A few people waved as we passed, recognizing me as a local and Des as the festival mascot.

"Beautiful morning, isn't it?" called Mrs. Boyko from Winnipeg, who'd set up an elaborate camping kitchen that would have impressed professional caterers.

"It is," I replied automatically. "Bodes well for a good aurora showing tonight."

Though my attention was increasingly focused on Des's behaviour. She pulled with the determined insistence that meant she'd locked onto something important.

She led me along the main lane toward the tent sites, her steps careful and deliberate. This wasn't curiosity or general interest—this was the focused approach of a dog following a specific trail.

Fern's tent started to come into view, and I started noticing details that didn't quite fit the peaceful morning scene. The complete stillness around her campsite, when most others showed signs of early morning activity. Other campers seemed to be giving that site a wide berth—whether by instinct or unease, I couldn't tell.

That's when I saw the figure in the lawn chair.

A figure sat by a cold campfire, utterly still in the pale

morning light. The position looked wrong somehow—too still, too slumped, lacking the natural micro-movements that come with sleep or rest. Even from a distance, my training was sending up warning signals.

Des whined softly, pressing against my leg as she stared at the still figure. Her whole body had gone tense in a way that told me whatever this was required immediate human attention.

I moved closer, noting more details that deepened my growing unease. A camping mug lay overturned on the ground nearby, its contents spilled and dried into a dark stain on the grass. The fire ring contained only cold ashes, though wisps of some lingering smell drifted from it—not just wood smoke, but something sharper and more unpleasant.

"Hello?" I called out, though something in the absolute stillness of the scene made my voice catch. "Everything alright?"

No response. Not even the slight shift or acknowledgment that comes when you wake someone who's been dozing.

I stepped closer, Des staying glued to my side as we approached. The smell sharpened—acrid, chemical, with a medicinal edge. It reminded me of hospital corridors, that antiseptic bite that made your nose burn and your throat close slightly.

That's when I saw the bright pink toque.

The familiar knitted hat that Fern wore everywhere during the festival sat perched on the figure's head, clearly visible even from several feet away. My heart clenched in instant recognition.

"Fern must have come back to her campsite," I thought, confusion flooding my chest.

Wait—Fern was supposed to be in the trailer. Why would she be back here?

The confusion deepened as I got closer and more details contradicted my initial assumption. The dark hair spilling out from under the bright pink knitted hat was wrong for Fern. The clothes were unfamiliar—a heavy sweater I didn't recognize, jeans that weren't Fern's style. The way the figure was positioned in the chair didn't match Fern's usual graceful posture.

Then it hit me—hard. Not Fern. Dawn.

Dawn Kessler sat motionless wearing Fern's characteristic pink toque, her body slumped in the lawn chair as though she'd nodded off beside the ashes. But the unnatural angle of her head, the way her arms had fallen, the complete absence of any movement—everything triggered every alarm my training had ever instilled.

The scene made awful, sudden sense. Dawn sleeping at Fern's campsite because they'd switched accommodations for the night. The toque must have been left behind when Fern moved to the trailer. Dawn sitting by the fire, perhaps unable to sleep, maybe enjoying the peaceful night atmosphere.

And then something had gone terribly wrong.

"Oh no," I whispered—unsure whether it was for Dawn or for what this meant for the town.

Des whined again, more urgently this time, her nose working as she processed scents I couldn't identify. She knew something was wrong here. She wasn't a trained K9,, but she recognized death when she met it.

I pulled out my phone with shaking hands, already backing away from the campsite as my mind processed the implications. Dawn—the woman I'd been so sure was behind the memorial disruption—was dead.

Which meant everything I thought I understood about this situation was wrong.

The phone rang twice before Jason answered, his voice

carrying the slightly irritated tone of someone who'd been hoping for a few more hours of sleep.

"Tilly? It's barely seven in the morning. This better be important."

"Jason." My voice was steadier than I expected, though I could hear the tension underneath. "I need you at the campground. Fern's campsite. We have a body."

His tone was changed instantly, the sleep vanished. "Are you sure?"

"I'm sure." I was still staring at Dawn's motionless form, at the pink toque that had initially fooled me into thinking this was our beloved astronomy enthusiast rather than the podcaster who'd arrived with such questionable timing. "It's Dawn Kessler. And Jason? It doesn't look like natural causes."

"Don't touch anything. Don't let anyone else near the scene. I'll be there in ten minutes."

As I waited for Jason to arrive, keeping watch over the campsite while Des sat alert beside me, one thought kept circling through my mind: maybe Dawn had been guilty of something, but had she stumbled into something too big for her to handle?

And maybe someone was afraid of her naming her source?

The morning sun continued to rise, painting the campground in increasingly golden light, but the peaceful festival atmosphere had already shifted into something darker. Other early risers were starting to notice that something was wrong, their voices becoming more subdued as they registered the tension around Fern's campsite.

Soon, everyone would know—the Aurora Nights Festival had claimed its first casualty. But the chemical smell, the unnatural stillness, the way Des had reacted—this didn't feel like an accident. Something about the scene whispered that Dawn's death wasn't the tragic mishap it appeared to be.

CHAPTER ELEVEN

I'd been guarding the scene for fifteen minutes when Jason arrived with the police tape. Des pressed anxiously against my legs while we watched him secure the perimeter. One of his deputies crouched near the fire pit, her camera clicking methodically as she documented the scene.

Around us, the festival atmosphere had already shifted. Word was spreading quickly through the campground—hushed conversations among early risers, the occasional nervous glance toward the billowing yellow tape. In the parking area, I could see at least three families loading cars with the brisk efficiency of people who'd decided their vacation was over.

"The festival ends in forty-eight hours," Jason said, following my gaze toward the departing families. "Once these tourists pack up and scatter to the wind, we'll lose any chance of finding witnesses."

The reality of Dawn's death was still settling in—the woman I'd been so certain was behind the memorial disruption, now lying motionless in that lawn chair, wearing Fern's bright pink toque.

"Her death looks suspicious," Jason said, his jaw tightening. "We're treating it as a crime scene until Major Crimes can get up here from Winnipeg and make the official determination. Nobody leaves until interviewed."

Des suddenly pulled toward the fire pit, whining at something in the ashes. The chemical smell lingered—faint but distinctive, like burned plastic with a sharp edge that made my nose itch.

"Did you notice the smell around the fire pit?" I said quietly. "Something doesn't seem right."

"The team will test everything," Jason said, making a note. "Tilly."

I turned to see Charlotte approaching, clipboard clutched to her chest and Charlie hovering protectively at her elbow. Her professional mask was firmly in place despite the early hour, but genuine shock flickered through her expression—the stunned disbelief of someone whose festival had just become a crime scene.

"Maybe you should sit down," Charlie suggested quietly, his hand hovering near Charlotte's elbow. "This is a lot to process."

"I'm fine," Charlotte said sharply, then immediately softened her tone. "Thank you, Charlie, but I need to handle this."

"This is terrible," Charlotte continued, her voice shaky. "Just terrible. That poor woman." She looked toward the campsite, then quickly away. "Do we know what happened?"

Jason's expression darkened as he surveyed the scene again. "Based on what I'm seeing here—the positioning of the body, the circumstances around the fire pit, that chemical smell—we're treating this as a suspicious death," Jason said firmly, watching both their reactions.

Charlie went very still. Charlotte's grip tightened visibly on her clipboard.

"Are you saying it could be murder?" Charlotte's voice cracked slightly. "How can you be certain? Couldn't it have been some kind of medical emergency?"

"That's what we need to determine," Jason said evenly. "Until Major Crimes arrives, we're securing the scene and interviewing everyone."

Charlotte's phone buzzed. She glanced at the screen, and I caught a flicker of anxiety that went beyond professional concern.

"Excuse me for a moment," she said, stepping away from our group. I strained to hear her hushed conversation: "Yes, I understand the situation is complicated... She did what she came to do. No, I can't discuss specifics right now. We'll have to talk later."

Charlie shifted to block our view, his casual stance a little too deliberate. When Charlotte returned, tucking her phone away with shaking hands, he stepped even closer.

"I'll need to draft a statement for the media," Charlotte said, her voice taking on a defensive edge. "This festival represents months of planning. The provincial tourism board will be asking questions, and I need to have answers."

"Let me handle the logistics," Charlie offered quickly. "You focus on the media and the board. I can cooperate with the police, help clean up before—"

"Before what?" Jason cut in sharply.

"Before the media gets here," Charlie said smoothly. "As soon as they catch wind of what happened, they'll be all over the place."

I watched the exchange with growing interest. Charlotte's phone call confirmed what I'd already suspected—Dawn's visit hadn't been coincidental at all. Charlotte had arranged her presence—for a reason. Meanwhile, Charlie's eagerness to "help" felt anything but harmless.

Before I could process further, something near Dawn's chair caught my eye—a gift bag, half hidden beneath the camp table.

"Jason," I called, pointing to the bag.

Jason approached, pulling on latex gloves. "Each campsite got one gift bag, from what I understand," he said, carefully lifting it to examine the tag. "Labelled with the primary camper's name." He turned the tag until "Fern" was visible, written in black marker.

"Dawn was staying here last night because she and Fern switched spots," I explained.

"What was in these bags?" Jason asked.

"Star charts, festival schedule, campfire colour packets, a packet of tea, a town pin, I think, and some business vouchers," I answered.

"Who had access to all this?" Jason asked.

"The whole volunteer crew," I said carefully. "We all handled the materials."

I could see Dawn's phone and small recording device on the camp table, the timestamp showing 11:47 p.m. "I saw Dawn use one of those flame packets last night," I said. "When Des and I walked past her campsite, she tossed a packet into the fire."

Charlie's gaze flicked to the gift bag in Jason's hands, his expression sharpening.

"Oh, stop," Charlotte said quickly, her voice tight with stress. "Practically every campground store in the country carries those—they're safe." She glanced between Charlie and Jason. "There has to be another explanation. What about the tea?"

"Where'd the tea come from?" Jason asked.

"Kelli's store," I said. "She put together a special blend for the festival."

"I'll look into it," Jason muttered, jotting down a few more notes.

More families were starting to pack up now. I spotted Mandy weaving through the crowd with thermoses and a tray of baked treats. Bertha peeled away from her, giving Mandy's arm a quick pat before heading my way.

"I called her," Bertha said quietly, appearing at my shoulder. "Figured we'd need her special touch to keep people calm."

Charlotte's phone buzzed again. This time she didn't answer it, but her hands trembled as she silenced it.

"I need to control the departures," Jason said, addressing both Charlotte and me. "People are starting to leave before we can interview them."

Charlotte's expression turned overwhelmed. "I have too many other things to do..." Her voice trailed off as her phone buzzed a third time.

"Let me handle this," Charlie offered again, his tone edging on urgent. "You've got enough on your plate."

"Tilly, could you station yourself at the campground gate?" Jason asked. "Explain the situation to anyone trying to leave. Let them know they need to speak with an officer first. I'll park a cruiser there so it looks official."

"And if they refuse?" I said.

Jason sighed. "I can't force them to stay. Just do whatever you can to convince them to stick around."

As we prepared to move away from the campsite, I couldn't shake what I'd just seen. Charlotte's phone call had suggested Dawn's presence here was orchestrated—"she did what she came to do." But by whom, and why?

Time was running out. We had forty-eight hours before the

festival ended and everyone scattered to the wind, taking their memories and potential testimony with them. Every departure car in the parking lot represented evidence walking away.

The campground gate was already backed up with vehicles when I arrived. Des stayed glued to my side while Jason's cruiser pulled into place to block the exit. A short line of cars had formed, drivers looking confused about why they couldn't just drive out.

"Good morning, everyone," I said, approaching the first car with a calm, steady smile. "I'm afraid departures will be delayed for a few hours this morning."

The driver—a man in a Maple Leafs jersey—rolled down his window. "What's going on? Why can't we leave?"

"The police need a quick word with everyone before you head out—they're looking into something that happened overnight." I kept my tone reassuring yet matter-of-fact. "They're setting up interviews at the campground office and should start within the hour. In the meantime, Mandy's got fresh coffee and cinnamon buns if you'd like breakfast while you wait."

"What kind of incident?" a woman in the passenger seat asked, concern creeping into her voice.

"Just something they need to document properly," I assured her. "You know how thorough police work can be."

As families reluctantly dispersed, I spotted Charlotte stood across the vendor area, phone pressed tight to her ear as she tried to smooth things over with whoever was on the other end. Charlie moved through the campsites with an easy smile, tossing out friendly waves and casual greetings as though nothing were amiss. Most people nodded back distractedly, busy with their own breakfasts or quiet conversations. Then he paused at one campsite where a family was clearly preparing to leave, their cooler already strapped to the roof of their SUV. His eager smile sharpened as he stepped closer.

"Let me give you a hand loading up."

Charlie caught my eye briefly, his helpful smile never wavering. The family thanked him, glad for the help. He held my gaze for just a beat too long—long enough for me to recognize it. He wasn't helping Jason's investigation at all. Maybe his efforts were meant for someone else. Then he turned back to the family, lifting their cooler with practiced ease.

My phone buzzed with a text from Callie: *Posted about road construction delays on socials to buy you some time. But Mom— someone's posting a string of comments that all sound the same— same phrases, different accounts.*

Before I could process that fully, a middle-aged woman approached me, looking anxious. "Excuse me—I wanted to tell someone. I saw something last night that might matter."

I immediately pulled out my phone to record. "What did you see?"

"I was up late reading and saw someone by that campfire that's been taped off around eleven. Wearing a pink hat—I assumed it was the astronomy lady at first, but when I looked closer the person seemed bigger somehow, different. And she must have gotten a bad packet of Aurora Fire—they were the strangest colour I've ever seen."

Another camper, overhearing, stepped forward. "I heard them talking about switching spots yesterday evening. The documentary lady said mentioned wanting to sleep under the stars, and the astronomy lady looked so relieved about getting a real bed."

A third voice joined in: "I walked my dog past there later in the evening and saw both ladies at the campsite together, organizing the switch. Very friendly about it. But that fire later —well, our flame packets paled next to hers."

"This is all important information," I said, making sure I had everyone's attention. "Please tell the police exactly what you just told me when they interview you."

Even as I spoke, I could see more cars edging around our stall tactics. Charlotte was fawning over the VIP guests while Charlie continued his suspiciously helpful luggage service.

"Tilly!" Fern's voice carried a note of distress. She hurried toward me, her face pale and eyes red-rimmed from crying. "I can't stop thinking about last night."

"Fern, I'm so sorry. This must be awful for you," I said gently.

"This is my fault. I should have been at my campsite." Her voice shook. "Dawn was so generous, offering her trailer just because I mentioned my back was killing me. And to know she was wearing my toque—she shook her head as if trying to clear the thought away. When I went back to the tent to grab a few essentials, I forgot my toque on the picnic table. It was so cold last night, I'm not surprised she grabbed whatever was there."

"You left your gift bag at the campsite." I asked, something clicking.

"Yes. No point in taking it with me. They're all the same, and if Dawn wanted something from mine, I could just swap the same from hers later." Fern's voice broke. "She died wearing my toque—using my things. If I hadn't complained about wanting a real bed..."

Before I could comfort Fern, Callie appeared at my elbow, tablet in hand and looking increasingly worried.

"Mom, the blog situation is getting worse. Someone's definitely manipulating the online conversation—posting identical comments from different accounts, all pushing the same narrative: that this was a 'tragic accident' and that 'speculation helps no one.'" She scrolled through the screen. "And underneath that, real people are spinning out with guesses—faulty lanterns, bad wiring, hidden grudges. It's turning messy."

"Can you moderate the comments?"

"I'm trying, but there are too many. And the coordinated ones—the ones shutting down discussion—they're coming faster now. This feels organized, not random." Callie showed me her screen. "Look at this—same exact phrase from five different accounts: 'Let's respect the family's privacy during this difficult time.' That's not how real people talk online."

"Someone's working hard to control the story," I said, studying the pattern.

"Exactly. And they're doing it professionally—not just random trolling. This feels organized."

Des pressed against my leg, sensing the tension. Around us, the joyful festival atmosphere was deteriorating rapidly. Vendors eyed their booths nervously while families clustered together in hushed conversations.

"Three families just cancelled their remaining camping reservations," Mabel announced breathlessly as she hurried up. "They said they're waiting to give their statement to the police then they're out. And there's a news van from Winnipeg setting up in the lot."

My phone buzzed with a text from Jason: *Major Crimes delayed until tomorrow morning. We're on our own.*

The message hit like cold water. No specialized forensics team—just Jason, his deputy, and whatever we could piece together before everyone scattered.

Across the festival area, I caught sight of Arlo avoiding eye contact with anyone, his usual confident demeanour replaced by nervous energy. He kept glancing toward the crime-scene tape around Fern's campsite, then looking away, his hands fidgeting with his astronomy-club clipboard—a man clearly uneasy about something.

Before I could investigate further, Charlotte appeared at my shoulder, her professional mask showing visible cracks.

"Perhaps we should consider cutting the festival short," she said, her voice strained. "Send everyone home before things get worse."

"That's exactly what we can't do," I said firmly. "Someone here knows something that could explain what really happened to Dawn."

But as I processed everything I'd learned—the witnesses who saw the strange flames, Fern's bag left at the campsite, the coordinated online campaign to call this an accident—pieces were starting to form a picture.

"The gift bags," I said slowly, mind racing. "At the crime scene, there was a gift bag with Fern's name on it."

Callie looked up from her tablet. "What about it?"

"Those gift bags are the key," I said said. "I'd bet whatever happened to Dawn started there."

I watched Charlie in the distance, still helping another family load their car. "Someone needs to start asking the right questions—before everyone disappears."

Around us, Aurora Nights was dying a quick death. But maybe—just maybe—we still had time to find the truth before it left with them.

CHAPTER TWELVE

The dismal morning had passed, and the festival grounds stretched before us, but everything felt wrong. Where there'd been brightness and bustle yesterday, today carried an unsettled quiet, the kind that creeps through a town after bad news travels faster than the wind. Even the fiddler at the bandstand seemed subdued, his bow scraping tentatively at a reel that refused to lift anyone's spirits.

I had managed a quick word with Jason after his initial interviews, and it seemed even more plausible that the gift bag had played a role in Dawn's death. I thought of everyone who'd been at the gift bag assembly. Charlotte (supervising), Charlie (coordinating), Arlo and Fern (star charts), Sean (provided flame packets), Mabel, and Kelli. I crossed off my own name with a thick black line.

Des pressed against my leg, trembling slightly—she'd been anxious since finding Dawn's body. "Forty-five hours," I muttered, checking my phone. "Less, actually. Some families already packing up."

I spotted Fern at her astronomy booth. She was standing a

little stiff, shoulders squared as though bracing against a storm, though the air was calm. The telescope gleamed, spotless, but no one leaned in to peer through it. A few locals lingered just outside the ropes — not close enough to be seen as interested, not far enough to avoid looking like they were watching.

I walked over, Des padding alongside me. She was attracting attention, too. A pair of girls crouched low to wave at her, whispering, "That's the dog from the video!" before darting away again. Callie trailed behind us, her camera hanging from her neck. She'd been snapping photos, but I could tell her heart wasn't in it.

Fern turned when I stopped at her booth. Her pink toque was missing. For a moment, I almost mentioned it before I remembering why. My throat went tight.

Fern fiddled with the telescope lens cap. The morning had gone quiet, the kind of hush that settled over crowds when unease spread and too many eyes were watching. "Quiet morning," she murmured, the words thin in the silence.

"Too quiet," I said.

She glanced up at me, eyes bright with unshed tears, then quickly away.

A couple walked past us, voices carrying just enough. "She was asking questions all over town," the man said. His wife shushed him, but her gaze slid toward Fern as they moved on.

I rested my hand on the edge of the table, steadying myself. "How are you holding up?"

Her hands twisted together, then stilled. "Everyone's staring."

"They're staring because they don't know what to think yet," I said.

She let out a shaky laugh. "Oh, they know what to think. They always do. They saw Dawn spending time with me... with

Arlo," she added, glancing away. "That's enough for people to start whispering."

Arlo. The name pulled me straight back to last night, to the shadowed shape of him approaching Dawn's trailer. To Fern answering the door, arms folded tight, her body blocking half the entrance. I hadn't heard their words, but I hadn't needed to. The tension had been written across both of them.

"Fern," I said quietly, "talk to me."

Her gaze flicked toward the telescope, as though it might rescue her. "Dawn was... curious. She asked a lot of questions, made people uncomfortable."

"Did she make you uncomfortable?"

Her shoulders stiffened. "What's that supposed to mean?"

"Only what it sounds like."

Her jaw clenched, then softened. "I envied her, maybe. She could walk into a space and take control. She was smart, fearless, and seemed like the type of person who always got what they wanted. People were drawn to her." I didn't know if Fern was aware of the bite in her tone. "Turns out, she wasn't a very nice person. She was only being nice until she got what she wanted." Her voice wavered. "But I didn't want her dead."

Behind us, Jason's steady voice carried from a knot of townsfolk. Calm, official, his RCMP tone in place. He was answering questions he couldn't really answer yet, saying things like "preliminary" and "still under review."

He glanced at me and pointed in the direction of the store. "Meet me in ten," he said. I nodded, and he turned back to the anxious faces around him.

Fern rubbed at her face. "They'll say I did it. That's what happens here, isn't it? They stitch together stories until they sound true."

I stayed quiet, weighing my next words. The pink toque flashed in my mind again, Fern handing over the gift bag, her offhand comment about her bad back. Put together the wrong way, it could look like more than it was.

"She was still young," I said softly. "If this was natural causes, it's unusual."

Her cheeks flushed. "So it wasn't natural?"

"I didn't say that."

"You didn't have to." She pressed her fists to her thighs, grounding herself. "You think I killed her."

"I think you're scared," I said, keeping my tone even.

Her gaze shot to mine, almost angry. "Of course I'm scared. She's dead, and I was the last one to see her." She stopped, staring past me toward Jason's steady voice in the distance. Her next words came out low, uncertain. "People will think it was me."

Her words made my chest tighten. Maybe they would.

I crouched a little, lowering my voice. "If there's something you know, Fern, tell me now. Before people decide for you."

Her eyes brimmed. She shook her head. "I can't."

A burst of laughter drifted from the next booth — children clamouring for sugar cookies Mandy had set out in an attempt to soften the morning. The sound felt out of step, like sunshine cutting across a shadowed room.

I straightened. "Then hold steady," I said. "Don't give them reason to twist this."

She nodded once, jerky, her face a map of worry.

As I turned away, my thoughts of Fern's pink toque and the memory of Arlo's shadow at that trailer door were interrupted by the sight of Charlotte across the parking lot, loading festival supplies into her car while talking rapidly on her phone. The same kind of urgent call she'd been taking at the crime scene. When Charlotte saw me watching, she ended the call abruptly.

I decided to start with her, before she disappeared into crisis-management mode.

Des whined when I stood too quickly, picking up on my frayed nerves.

Charlotte's shoulders tightened when she saw me approaching. "I've already given Jason my statement. Twice."

"I know. I'm just trying to understand the timeline."

"The timeline of what? Dawn's death? The festival falling apart?" Charlotte's voice had an edge of hysteria.

"The gift bags," I said carefully. "After I left the assembly yesterday, did anyone come back? Ask to check specific bags?"

Charlotte slammed her car trunk. "How would I know? I'm supervising fifty volunteers and almost as many projects, not running surveillance."

"But you had the master list. You were tracking everything."

"Charlie was tracking. I was managing." Charlotte's phone buzzed. She silenced it without looking. "The bags were loaded into boxes and a few people helped carry them to the campground for Fern and Charlie to distribute." Charlotte turned defensive. "Why are you asking me this instead of Charlie? He handled the logistics."

I pushed: "You assigned him that role. Did he report anything unusual?"

"Charlie's always been helpful. Unlike some people who come and go as they please." The accusation hung between us.

I hesitated. Jason had mentioned that Arlo admitted, during his interview, to dropping a box during the gift bag assembly—one of those 'don't-repeat-this' details. But Charlotte had been right there that day. If she'd seen it herself, maybe I could read her reaction.

"Did anyone specifically handle the flame packets after Arlo dropped that box?"

Charlotte's eyes snapped up, the flicker of surprise gone

almost before it formed. "Interesting question," she said slowly. "Jason must be sharing more than he should."

My pulse stumbled. *Too far.*

"I just meant—"

"I know what you meant." Charlotte's phone rang once more. This time she looked at it, and her face paled. "I have to take this."

She turned away, but I caught fragments: "Yes, I understand... No, nothing definitive... The forensics team hasn't yet arrived..."

When Charlotte turned back, her professional mask was firmly in place. "If you want to investigate someone, talk to Arlo. He was acting strange all day. Dropped that packed box of flame packets, hands shaking, then insisted on cleaning it up himself—very thorough for someone who seemed eager to leave."

"Charlotte—"

"I have three reporters calling and a tourism board demanding answers. Unless you have real questions instead of fishing expeditions, we're done."

She slid into her car but paused, hand on the door. "Arlo was jumpy around Dawn from the moment she arrived. Ask him why."

I found Charlie helping an elderly couple load their camper. He didn't stop moving when he saw me.

"Tilly! Seems as if you're making the rounds. Happy to talk while I help these folks."

Des growled low.

"Charlie, you coordinated the entire gift bag assembly. You must remember who handled what."

"Community effort!" He was lifting a cooler, forcing me to follow. "Everyone pitched in."

"But you were tracking everything."

"Just making sure every bag got all components. Charlotte's very particular." He'd moved to adjusting the couple's bike rack. "Can't have incomplete bags."

I tried to pin him down: "After Arlo dropped those packets, you offered to help. Did he say anything?"

"Very nervous. Sweating. Kept checking his phone." Charlie didn't make eye contact. "Almost like he was in a hurry."

He paused to tighten a knob on their roof rack. "Always happy to help," he said to the couple.

The elderly woman thanked Charlie profusely. He beamed, then scanned the area for other places to lend a hand.

"Charlie, stop moving and talk to me properly."

"People are on edge, Tilly. Don't want them leaving without a friendly face trying to make things a little better for them." He was already greeting the next family. "You should talk to Arlo. Got annoyed when I stepped in to help." Charlie gave his helpful smile. "I really must help these folks now."

He effectively dismissed me, already deep in conversation about the best route to avoid traffic. I watched him gesture animatedly as he helped another family, his performance of helpfulness so polished it bordered on choreography.

The pattern was obvious: Everyone wanted me to focus on Arlo. Either he was guilty—or someone wanted me to think so. But Fern's demeanour concerned me just as much.

"I know she's hiding something," I told Des, my voice barely above a whisper. "I just don't know what it is."

My phone buzzed with a text from Callie: *Mom URGENT. I'm on my way to the store. Blog exploded. Everything's worse.*

Des whined, pulling toward the store with unusual insistence. She'd been doing that more lately—guiding me away from things that felt wrong. A sinking feeling told me whatever waited at the store might be the final nail in this investigation's coffin.

The store felt eerily quiet when I pushed through the door, Des padding beside me. Normally by this time of morning we'd have a steady stream of festival-goers looking for forgotten supplies or local curiosities. Today, the silence felt oppressive.

I nodded to Parker behind the counter, noticing his pale face and quiet expression. "Everything okay?" After a few years of working as the store's regular stock boy, Parker was more than capable of handling the store on his own when Callie, Bertha, or I couldn't be here, but these weren't normal circumstances.

His face looked blank for just a second until he shook it off after hearing the concern in my voice.

"Yeah, everything's fine, Tilly. It's just... it's a weird day, right?"

"You said it. If you want to leave, I can take over," I said as I shed my coat.

"Nah, I'm fine. Really. Jason's in the back waiting for you, by the way."

The phone rang and I started to circle back to grab it, but Parker waved me off. "You're busy. I got it."

Jason leaned against the counter in the back room, arms crossed, a weariness in his shoulders that no amount of uniform starch could disguise. He'd loosened his tie and unbuttoned his collar—a rare concession that showed just how wrung out he was.

I slid into the chair opposite him and rubbed at the knot in my neck. "Fern's hiding something."

Jason's brow arched, but he didn't answer right away. That was his style—let the silence do the work, make me fill it.

"She's too... jumpy," I pressed. "She hedged every answer, danced around simple questions. And the toque—"

Jason held up a hand. "Tilly—"

"—the toque," I barrelled on. "Dawn was wearing it. Fern was known for that pink toque, and suddenly Dawn has it. And don't forget Arlo visiting Dawn's trailer. That wasn't just a friendly drop-in."

Jason exhaled slowly through his nose. "You're tying loose threads into a noose. Careful where you throw it, or you'll hang the wrong person."

His words stung, maybe because they weren't entirely wrong.

I leaned back, folding my arms tight against my chest. "You didn't see her, Jase. Fern was nervous in a way that didn't read like grief. She was dodging me."

Jason pushed off the counter and came to sit opposite me. The old metal chair groaned under his weight. "You know what people do when they're nervous? They ramble. They forget what they said two minutes ago. They try to fill silences. You're reading it like a suspect interview. I'm reading it like a woman who just lost someone she admired and is scared she'll be next."

I hated how often he made sense.

Still, I shook my head. "She brought Dawn that gift bag herself—all but shoved it into her hands. Encouraged her to use those campfire colour packets that same night."

"Which makes her enthusiastic about festival swag, not a killer." Jason's eyes softened, but his voice stayed firm. "Tilly, you're forcing connections because you want an answer. That's not the same as having one."

I bristled. "What about Arlo? Showing up at Dawn's trailer late at night, looking guilty as sin. Fern opening the door like she didn't want him there. You can't tell me that doesn't mean something."

Jason rubbed a hand down his jaw. "Arlo complicates

things, sure. But showing up at her trailer doesn't prove guilt. People do strange things when they're under stress. Until we know more, it's just another piece of the puzzle—not the whole picture."

I opened my mouth, then closed it again. The words wouldn't form, only the gnawing sense that I was losing my grip on the story I'd been building.

Des shifted, letting out a small whine that broke the tension. I reached down and brushed her ear between my fingers. She leaned into the touch, steady as always.

Jason's voice gentled. "Look, I know you feel like you have to carry this. That you're the one who sees the patterns everyone else misses. And sometimes you do. But you've also got blind spots. Fern's an easy target because she looks like she's hiding something. But sometimes hiding's just surviving."

I stared at him. "You think I'm wrong."

"I think you might be making Fern look guiltier than she is. And if the wrong person hears that..." He trailed off, and I didn't need him to finish—the Bugles.

Jason must have read my face because he added, "If the Bugles catch even a hint of Fern being tied up in this, they'll spin it however they want. They'll use it to discredit her, the astronomy club, LANTERN's support of the festival, maybe even the festival itself. CLAIM would love that."

I blew out a breath, the knot in my chest tightening. "The Bugles don't sit still. If they're quiet, it's because they're already spinning it."

Jason nodded once. "Exactly—and that's why I'm not giving them ammunition."

My throat tightened, but I pushed back. "So what—sit on my hands and do nothing?"

Jason leaned forward, elbows on his knees. "No. But

chasing half-formed theories and pressing people until they break? That's not helping. It just makes more noise for the Bugles to use against us. You're good at this, Til—but not every loose thread needs pulling."

I looked down at my hands, fingers clenched in my lap. My SAR instincts had always been my compass. They'd gotten me out of storms, through tangled woods, across impossible terrain. But here? Every trail I found dissolved beneath my feet.

"I can't just stop," I whispered.

Jason's sigh was heavy but not unkind. "I'm not asking you to stop being you. I'm asking you to think about what your digging does to the people you're trying to protect."

Silence stretched, Des's slow breaths the only sound. I wanted to argue, to fight back with the certainty I used to carry like armour. But all I had left was doubt.

Finally, I nodded, though it felt like conceding more than I wanted. "Fine. I'll... ease off."

Jason studied me for a long moment, then leaned back, his chair scraping softly across the floor. "Good. Let me handle the official side until we get tox results back. Then we'll know what we're really dealing with."

I forced a thin smile, one he probably saw right through. "Sure. Leave it to the professionals."

He didn't rise to the bait. Just gave me a steady look that said, *I've got this. Let it go.*

When he left a few minutes later, the store felt emptier than ever. I sat there long after the door clicked shut, stroking Des's ears, trying to make sense of the hollow ache his words had left behind.

He was right—and that meant I was wrong. Again.

And if I was wrong about Fern... where did that leave me?

The back door banged open just as the bell jingled after Jason.

"Mom, I tried to do the right thing. I made everything worse." Callie yanked from her bag and flipped it open on the desk.

I moved around the counter to see her screen. The blog post was titled "Truth and Exploitation: Dawn Kessler's Pattern" in her clean, professional font.

"I researched everything," Callie said, her voice thick with tears. "Three other towns where Dawn showed up during tragedies. Always with 'perfect timing.' Always turning grief into content. I thought if I laid out the facts, people would see she had a pattern—and that what happened here wasn't necessarily on us."

The post was careful, factual. No wild speculation, just documented patterns laid out with journalistic precision. It ended with: *We deserve to mourn without becoming content.*

"This is good journalism," I started, but she was already shaking her head.

"Look at the comments."

She refreshed the page. *147 comments.*

Victim blaming at its finest.

Small town cover-up confirmed.

What are they hiding?

Another refresh. *203 comments.*

Why is the store owner's family controlling the narrative?

Daughter protecting mommy's illegal investigation.

Then I saw the one that made my blood run cold:

Jason McKay sharing evidence with his sister. Conflict of interest much?

"Someone knows exactly how to weaponize this story," Callie whispered. "They're using my ethics against us."

I scrolled through more comments, watching the narrative spiral. Someone had already linked a popular true-crime forum, speculating about Dawn's death under the thread: *Small Town Secrets: What Really Happened to Dawn Kessler?*

"We're trending," Callie said, the word heavy with disgust. "Parker texted me and said the store phone won't stop ringing. Three reporters have called in the last hour."

Then she broke down completely. "I became exactly what Dawn was—using tragedy for content. Grandpa would've been ashamed of me."

"No," I said firmly, pulling her into my arms. "You tried to set the record straight with facts. Someone else twisted it."

But even as I comforted her, I was scanning the comments for anything useful. That's when I saw the cluster that made everything click:

Ask why Arlo Trent was at Dawn's trailer at midnight.

Three witnesses saw him there.

Looking angry when he left.

Multiple accounts confirming the same timeline. Combined with Charlotte and Charlie both pointing toward him and my own observations last night, the blog comments suddenly felt like the final piece of evidence I'd been waiting for.

"I need to talk to Arlo," I said, already moving for the door. "Now."

Callie grabbed my hand. "Mom, hang on. Let's think this through."

It was good advice, but it didn't change the fact that the trail of crumbs pointed to Arlo.

"Either he's guilty," I said, "or someone really wants me to believe he is. I need to hear it from him."

"Mom, please—"

But I was already out the door, Des followed reluctantly, whining louder with each step as we headed back toward the festival grounds.

CHAPTER THIRTEEN

I found Arlo near the edge of the festival grounds, standing apart from the crowd with his hands shoved deep in his jacket pockets. His easy-going demeanour had evaporated, replaced by something that looked like barely contained panic. He kept glancing toward the campground, then quickly looking away.

"Arlo," I called softly.

He turned, and I saw the strain written across his features. His eyes were red-rimmed, and his usual smile was nowhere to be found.

Oh—Tilly." He rubbed the back of his neck. "This sure is something, isn't it?"

"It is." I stopped a few feet away. "You look like you haven't slept."

He let out a shaky laugh. "Didn't, really. Long night."

"You seem rattled," I said, keeping my voice even.

"Everyone is," he replied, but his voice was strained.

"I saw you last night, Arlo. Around eleven-thirty. You were heading toward the campground."

His face went pale. "I... I was just..."

"Just what?"

He glanced around nervously. "Just checking on things. You know, making sure everything was secure for the night."

"That's not what it looked like." I kept my voice gentle but persistent. "It looked like you were going somewhere specific. To see someone specific."

Arlo's shoulders sagged slightly. "I don't know what you think you saw."

"I think you went to see Dawn Kessler. The question is why."

"Why would I want to see her?" But the defensive tone gave him away.

"That's what I'm asking you."

He was quiet for a long moment, staring at the ground. When he finally looked up, there was something desperate in his eyes. "It's... complicated."

"Most things are. Try me."

Another silence stretched. He shifted his weight, pushed his glasses up his nose, and opened his mouth twice before words actually came. At last, so quietly I had to lean in to hear: "We met at a conference."

"What kind of conference?"

"A science conference in Toronto." Each word sounded stiff, like he was giving a deposition instead of a memory. "A few years back."

"And?"

"And we... uh... spent some time together." His ears went red. "Just a weekend. I thought we'd... connected."

The way he said it—awkward, bitter, like he still couldn't believe he'd let himself think it meant something—told me there was more beneath it. "But?"

"But I was wrong about her character." His hands were clenched into fists now. "She was using me."

"How?"

"I shared my research with her. Ideas I'd been working on for months. Preliminary findings about aurora prediction patterns." His voice got stronger as his anger took over. "Thought I was impressing her with my work."

"What happened?"

"The next day, she presented my ideas as her own insights during a panel discussion. Made me look like a fool when I tried to correct her, laughed it off like I was some amateur who didn't understand my own research."

Now we were getting somewhere. "That must have been humiliating."

"Devastating. Career-damaging. And when I confronted her privately afterward, she told me I should be grateful for the learning experience. Said maybe next time I'd think twice before trying to impress someone out of my league."

The bitterness in his voice was palpable. Resentment, crystallized into something hard and sharp.

"So when she showed up at our committee meeting..."

"I panicked. But I thought—hoped—that maybe she'd forgotten about me. That she wouldn't even remember our weekend."

"But she did remember."

"Oh, she remembered everything. Made a point of cornering me yesterday, asking if I was still 'playing around with amateur astronomy.'" His voice mimicked her tone with obvious contempt. "Wanted to know if I'd learned to keep my brilliant theories to myself."

The picture was getting clearer, and uglier. "So last night you decided to do something about it."

He nodded. "I went to ask her to keep quiet about our history. I didn't want..." He trailed off.

"Didn't want what?"

He hesitated, dragging a hand across the back of his neck. His eyes flicked toward the ground, then back at me, pained. It was the look of someone caught between protecting himself and protecting someone else. Finally, his voice dropped, almost apologetic: "I've been seeing someone. Someone local. I didn't want Dawn stirring up trouble."

"Fern."

His head snapped up. "How did you—"

"It's a small town, Arlo. People notice things." Though in truth, I was putting pieces together from the way they'd interacted, the protective way Fern had spoken about him. "How long?"

"A few months. We've kept it quiet because..." He gestured helplessly. "Fern values her privacy. And you know how people talk."

"And Fern didn't know about Dawn."

"There was no reason to tell her. It was ancient history."

"Except Dawn showed up and made it current events."

"I just wanted to keep her away from Fern. To make sure she didn't poison what we have with her version of what happened between us."

I felt a chill as the implications settled in. "So you went to her trailer last night."

"Yeah, but Dawn wasn't there. Fern was. They'd switched places—Dawn was camping at Fern's site, and Fern was using the trailer."

That explained the tension I'd witnessed between Arlo and Fern at the trailer door. "What happened?"

"Fern started asking questions I couldn't answer. Not

without explaining about Dawn and me." His voice cracked. "So I told her everything."

"How did she take it?"

"About as well as you'd expect. She was furious, not just about my history with Dawn, but about me keeping it secret after she arrived in town. She got angry. Said maybe I deserved what happened at that conference if I was stupid enough to trust someone like that. She wasn't herself."

The pieces were starting to fit together in ways I didn't like. Arlo had access… and more than enough reason to be angry.

"Did you ever actually see Dawn last night?"

"No. After the argument with Fern, I just went home—mostly to stare at the ceiling." His shoulders sagged. "I should have gone to find Dawn at the campsite, should have had that conversation I'd planned. Maybe if I had…"

"Maybe if you had, what?"

"Maybe she'd still be alive."

I stared at him, weighing his words, his body language, the story he'd just told me. It was possible he was telling the truth—that he'd gone home after the argument with Fern, leaving Dawn alive at the campsite. But it was also possible he was lying, that he had found Dawn and decided to settle the score once and for all.

"Arlo," I said carefully, "you realize how this looks."

"I know." His voice was barely a whisper. "But I didn't hurt her, Tilly. I swear I didn't."

"Then why do you still look like a man hiding something?"

He didn't answer—just turned and walked away, shoulders hunched under the weight of whatever secrets he was carrying.

Watching him go, I realized I'd never really seen him—the quiet man cataloguing constellations while a storm brewed inside. He was a man with history he'd hidden, grudges he'd carried, and a relationship he'd buried deep because Fern had wanted it that way. And Dawn had just brought all of it back to the surface.

The humiliation, the resentment, the threat of exposure. Arlo had every reason to want her gone.

I pulled out my phone and started typing a text to Jason, then stopped. If I went to Jason now with just this conversation, Arlo might deny it while he worked to protect his and Fern's relationship. Without more concrete evidence, it would be my word against his.

I needed to find a way to get the whole truth. And Arlo was clearly too comfortable keeping his secrets in private conversations. Maybe it was time to make this less private.

The festival's afternoon crowd had gathered near the bandstand, where musicians were setting up for an impromptu concert meant to lift everyone's spirits. Children chased each other between the vendors while their parents clutched coffee cups and spoke in hushed tones about what had happened. The normalcy felt forced, like a bandage over a wound that wouldn't stop bleeding.

I spotted Arlo near the edge of the crowd, staring at his phone with the same haunted expression he'd worn during our conversation. He looked isolated, separate from the families enjoying the music.

As I approached, he was digging through his backpack with increasing frustration, muttering about misplaced observation notes. "I know I put them in here somewhere..." The bag tilted as he pulled it toward him, and loose change scattered across the ground between us. Quarters, loonies, and something that caught the light differently.

"Sorry," he said, dropping to gather the coins. "Seems to only happen when I'm in a hurry."

I bent to help, my fingers closing around a silver dollar before I really looked at it. Then I froze.

The coin was heavy in my palm, pristine despite its age. A 1967 silver dollar with the distinctive die crack across the wolf's ear that Dad had pointed out to me dozens of times. His prize piece.

"Where did you get this?" The words came out sharper than intended.

Arlo glanced up from collecting the other coins, his hand stilling when he saw what I was holding. "Oh. That." He straightened slowly. "I found it."

"You found it." I turned the silver dollar over, studying the reverse crack. "A 1967 howling wolf silver half dollar with a die error. You just found it."

"Near the community centre, yesterday morning."

The other coins were still scattered around us, but I could see them clearly now. A 1965 quarter, also silver. A commemorative loonie from 1987. The exact combination I'd helped Dad arrange in the display case.

"These are from the memorial box." My voice sounded distant. "These are Dad's collection coins."

Arlo blinked, colour draining from his face. For a beat he just stared, as if the weight of what I'd said had only just landed. "Tilly, I—I didn't realize..."

"You stole the box." The realization hit like cold water. "You're the one who took it."

Arlo's face went pale. "No, that's not... I didn't steal anything."

For a split second I wanted to believe him. Wanted to think there was some simple, harmless reason he had those coins. But then everything lined up—the missing box, the argument at the trailer, his annoyance over dropping the Aurora Fire box, his confession about Dawn and Fern. It was too neat to be coincidence. The sympathy I'd felt walking over here iced over in an instant. This wasn't a misunderstanding. Arlo Trent had crossed a line, and every instinct in me screamed that he was behind it all.

My pulse was racing, reason trailing behind. Still, the words came out before I could stop them—"You set Dawn up. You told her about the memorial, gave her wrong information to make sure she'd disrupt it. Then while everyone was dealing with that chaos, you took the box."

"You don't understand—"

"And Dawn probably figured it out. After you had that argument with Fern last night, what did you do to Dawn?"

Arlo scrambled to his feet, leaving the remaining coins scattered. "Tilly, stop. You're jumping to conclusions."

"Am I?" I stood too, the silver dollar warm in my fist. "You've got Dad's coins in your pocket, you set up the memorial disruption, and now Dawn's dead."

"That's not what happened!" His voice cracked, rising above the ambient festival noise.

"Then why are you carrying stolen coins? Why did you conceal the fling you two had at that conference in Toronto?"

A collective gasp rippled through the small crowd that had gathered, followed by a rising hum of whispers. I caught sight of the Balsam Belles near the bandstand, their eyes practically shining with scandal.

"Did she just say fling?" Nora gasped, hand flying to her chest for emphasis.

"With the dead podcaster?" Trish added, eyes wide and voice rich with glee. "Well, that explains the haunted look he's been wearing."

"My word," Enid said, leaning in as though she couldn't

possibly look away. "And here we thought he was only married to his school books and telescope."

"I didn't steal them!" The desperation in his voice was drawing even more attention. "I found them scattered behind the community centre. I was going to return them, but then Dawn died and everything went crazy."

"Convenient story." My own voice was getting louder, anger overriding caution. "You orchestrated the whole thing. Used Dawn to create chaos so you could rob the memorial, and when she figured out what you'd done—"

"She didn't figure out anything because there was nothing to figure out!" Arlo's hands were shaking. "I found those coins. I was going to do the right thing."

Our raised voices had created a circle of onlookers. I could see phones coming out, people recognizing the drama unfolding.

"Wait," a familiar voice called from the crowd. An older man from the hardware store stepped forward, squinting at the scattered coins. "Is that Walter's coin collection?"

The murmur through the gathering crowd was electric. Now everyone understood what they were looking at.

"Those are from Walter's memorial," someone else confirmed. "The ones that went missing."

"Stop!" Fern's voice cut through the crowd as she pushed her way toward us, her face flushed with panic. "What's going on? Why is everyone staring?"

She looked between me and Arlo, taking in his pale face and the coins scattered on the ground. "Arlo, what are those?"

"They're from the memorial box," I said before he could answer. "He's been carrying them around since yesterday. And he lied about knowing Dawn—they had a fling a few years back that ended badly. But you knew that already, didn't you, Fern?"

Fern's colour rose, her voice sharp with conviction. "That's impossible. Arlo would never steal from Walter's memorial. Tell them, Arlo."

"I didn't steal anything," Arlo said miserably. "But I can't prove it."

"Then why were you carrying my dad's coins?" I pressed. "How do you explain that?"

His mouth opened, then closed again. He dragged a hand across the back of his neck, his face tightening. "Because when I picked them up, I looked up and saw Dawn across the way. She... blew me a kiss."

The Balsam Belles all went wide-eyed, gasping in unison like they'd just been handed front-row tickets to the drama.

"Not sweet—mocking," Arlo added quickly, colour flooding his face as if he'd realized exactly how it sounded. "And just then Fern walked past. I was terrified she'd seen it. I froze. I forgot all about the coins after that."

The ripple of shock through the crowd was immediate. Whispered conversations started, people putting pieces together, and the Belles leaned in like bloodhounds on a scent.

"Did he just say Dawn blew him a kiss?" Nora gasped.

"And he was concerned Fern would see it?" Trish said, wide-eyed.

"My word," Enid breathed. "The poor man's been living a soap opera and we didn't even know it."

Fern's face went white, then red. "Arlo—"

"I didn't steal anything," he repeated, voice cracking. "But after that, I couldn't think straight. I knew I had to talk to Dawn before she did something that Fern would notice. Confrontation isn't my thing, everyone knows that. I was so nervous that at the gift bag assembly I dropped the box because my hands were shaking. But I finally worked up the courage late last night. I went to Dawn's trailer to confront her. To tell her to stop playing games, stop risking everything."

He faltered, his gaze cutting toward Fern, panic flickering there. "But it wasn't Dawn who answered the door. It was Fern. And I had to explain why I was there."

The silence thickened. Arlo's face crumpled under the weight of it, the pressure of so many eyes. The words tumbled out before he could stop them.

"I told her there'd been... a fling with Dawn. That it was over. That Dawn meant nothing. Because the only person who matters is Fern. We've been together for months."

The ripple of whispers sharpened to an audible buzz. I caught sight of the Belles again, leaning forward like hens at a feed trough.

"Did he just say they were together?" Nora whispered, loud enough for half the crowd to hear.

"For months?" Trish added, eyes gleaming.

Enid pressed a hand to her chest. "Oh, this is better than costume bingo night."

Fern looked like she wanted to disappear into the ground.

The crowd erupted in excited chatter. This was gossip gold —the nerdy science teacher and the quiet museum worker, secretly dating, now connected to an affair, theft, and murder.

Fern's face went white, then red. "Arlo, how could you—"

But I wasn't done. The pieces were falling into place too clearly to stop. "That's a convenient story, Arlo."

"What?" Fern gasped. "Tilly, what are you saying?"

"I'm saying your boyfriend had motive to keep Dawn quiet. She probably figured out he was the one who set her up for the memorial disruption. Maybe she even caught him with the stolen coins. And he was terrified she'd expose their fling to you, Fern. So he silenced her."

"That's crazy!" Arlo's voice cracked. "I would never hurt anyone!"

"Wouldn't you? You've been lying about everything else. The theft, your relationship with Dawn, your relationship with Fern." I looked directly at him. "What else are you lying about, Arlo? What really happened at that campsite?"

The crowd had grown larger, drawn by the escalating drama. I could see Charlotte at the edge, her expression calculating, and Charlie moving closer as if sensing an opportunity.

"Oh my," Charlotte's voice carried clearly as she stepped into view, her expression a perfect mix of shock and concern. "This is quite a development. I had no idea there was so much... complexity surrounding our festival."

Charlie appeared beside her. "This looks serious. Should someone call the police?"

The circle around us swelled until it pressed tight against the vendor stalls; phones flashed like fireflies.

"Everyone needs to step back." Jason's authoritative voice cut through the chaos as he pushed through the crowd. The noise swelled—voices overlapping, phones raised, the air thick with heat and accusation. Des whined low, uneasy.

His eyes took in the scattered coins, Arlo's guilty expression, and Fern's tears. "What happened?"

"He's got Walter's coins," I said, holding up the silver dollar. "From the memorial box."

Jason crouched to examine the scattered change, his expression grim. "Arlo, you want to explain this?"

"I found them," Arlo said, voice thin. "I was going to bring them back, but then Dawn—then everything—went wrong."

Jason stood, his jaw tight. He began collecting the coins carefully. "These need to be processed properly."

The crowd began to disperse as Jason took control, but the

damage was done. I could see people clustering in small groups, phones out, already sharing what they'd witnessed.

Jason took my arm firmly once the immediate area had cleared. "With me. Now."

He guided me away from the lingering onlookers to a quieter area near the parking lot. When we were out of earshot, his expression was thunderous.

"What the heck was that?"

"He had Dad's coins, Jason. The proof that he—"

"The proof that he what? Had coins in his possession? That's not proof of murder, Tilly. That's barely proof of theft if his story about finding them holds up."

My confidence wavered. "But the timing, the way he's been acting—"

"The way he's been acting is like someone scared and in over his head. Not necessarily like a killer." Jason shook his head. "Do you realize what you just did? You turned a private investigation into a public spectacle."

I looked back toward where Fern was standing with a small group of women, their voices low but their glances sharp. She looked devastated, exposed.

"Fern's not just a person of interest anymore," Jason continued. "She's the centre of town gossip. Now everyone knows she's secretly dating someone who had a past with a murdered woman—a guy you just accused of murder in front of half the town. You've made her look complicit by asso-ciation."

The reality of what I'd done started sinking in. "I didn't mean to expose their relationship."

"But you did. And worse, you've given people like Charlotte all the ammunition they need." He gestured toward where Charlotte was speaking quietly with a small group, her phone in her hand. "Look at her. She's already spinning this."

Charlotte's voice carried clearly: "I just think people deserve to know the kind of people who support LANTERN. This level of—drama—surrounding them."

"I was trying to get answers," I said weakly.

"By making accusations you couldn't prove by turning private pain into public entertainment. Isn't that what you were accusing Dawn of doing?" Jason's disappointment was worse than his anger. "Tilly, sometimes your version of help is what puts people in the most danger."

I watched Fern walking quickly toward her car, her shoulders hunched with shame. The whispers followed her like a wake, and I realized how completely I'd misjudged everything.

I'd been so certain that the coins were the smoking gun, that confronting Arlo would force some kind of confession. Instead, I'd exposed an innocent woman's private life, connected her to a murder investigation in the most damaging way possible, and handed her enemies everything they needed to destroy her reputation.

"The coins don't prove he killed Dawn," I admitted quietly.

"No, they don't. They raise questions about the memorial box theft, sure. But murder? That's a much bigger leap, and you made it in front of half the town."

As Jason walked away to deal with the evidence and the aftermath, I stood alone in the parking lot, watching the festival continue around me. People were still talking about what they'd witnessed, the story growing with each telling.

I'd wanted to protect Fern, to find answers, to solve the mystery. Instead, I'd made everything infinitely worse for the one person who least deserved it.

And somewhere behind the festival music, I could almost hear the sound of everything I'd just broken.

CHAPTER FOURTEEN

Later that afternoon, the store was quiet except for the hum of the refrigerator and Des's soft breathing. I'd sent Parker home an hour ago, flipped the sign to "Closed," but I couldn't bring myself to actually leave. Instead, I'd been rearranging the same shelf of camping supplies for twenty minutes, moving things that didn't need to be moved.

"Mom." Callie's voice cut through my fog. "Sit down."

"I'm fine."

"You're spiralling." She grabbed my arm and steered me toward the bench by the window—the spot where customers waited while I rang up purchases, where Walter used to sit with his coffee and watch the street outside. "Des, help me out here."

Des immediately trotted over and pressed her nose against my knee, those brown eyes full of concern.

I sank onto the bench. My hands were shook slightly. "Jason was right. I made everything worse."

"Jason *was* mad. There's a difference." Callie sat beside me, close enough that our shoulders touched. "And yeah, today was a disaster. But sitting here beating yourself up about it isn't solving anything."

"I don't know what I'm doing anymore." The admission came out raw. "I thought I had it figured out. The coins, Arlo's history with Dawn, the timeline—it all seemed to fit. And then it just... fell apart."

Des nudged my hand until I scratched behind her ears. The familiar motion helped, a little.

"Remember what you used to say?" Callie's voice softened, "When you got stuck on a trail?"

I did know. The words had been drilled into me during countless SAR training sessions, repeated whenever I fixated too hard on a single clue. "*Patterns reveal themselves when you stop staring at one square inch of ground.*"

"Right. So maybe stop staring at Arlo—and those coins." She shifted to face me more directly. "Step back. Look at the whole picture."

I closed my eyes, trying to quiet the noise in my head—Jason's disappointment, the crowd's shocked faces, Fern's devastation. Trying to see past my own mistakes to what was actually there.

Des shifted, resting her chin on my knee with a soft whine. The memory surfaced unbidden—Des at Dawn's campsite that morning, nose working overtime at the cold fire pit. That small, uneasy sound she made when something smelled wrong.

"The fire," I said slowly.

Callie waited.

"When Des and I found Dawn, she went straight to the fire pit. Kept sniffing it, whining." I opened my eyes. "She knew something was off about it."

"Dogs can smell things we can't."

"And I saw it burning the night before. When I walked past

after talking to Dawn." The image came back—strange colours dancing above the logs, that sharp chemical smell cutting through the wood smoke. "The flames weren't normal—wrong, somehow."

"Wrong how?"

"Just different. Brighter in some places—this vivid turquoise colour mixed with orange." I stood up, needing to move. "At the time I thought it was just those campfire colour packets everyone was using. But now..."

"Now?"

Something was surfacing, just out of reach. A conversation, a detail I'd dismissed as irrelevant. "At the museum—when Sean was setting up his displays."

"What about it?"

"He was frustrated. Said specimens kept going missing all week." I paced to the window, watching the October dusk settle over Main Street.

Callie's expression shifted slightly. "Okay."

"He said something else too. When Charlie was asking about heating minerals." The memory crystallized—Sean's voice in the museum hall, the careful way he'd explained the chemistry. "*Fluorite releases a gas when you heat it.*" The words hung between us.

"And?" Callie prompted gently.

"And you definitely don't want to breathe those fumes—they're deadly toxic." I turned back to face her. "That's what Sean said. Deadly toxic."

Callie was quiet for a long moment. "So you're thinking the missing samples and Dawn's weird flames might be connected."

"I don't know." The frustration leaked through. "Maybe. But even if they are, I can't see how they connect. Someone steals minerals from the museum—then what? How does it end up in Dawn's fire?"

"The gift bags," Callie said slowly. "Those Aurora Fire packets."

"But everyone got the same packets—from the same supplier, with identical contents." I shook my head. "Unless…"

"Unless someone tampered with them."

The possibility settled uncomfortably. "But that would mean someone had access to the bags *before* they were distributed. Someone at the assembly."

"Which was, basically, half the town." Callie pulled out her tablet, fingers moving quickly. "You, me, Charlotte, Charlie, Mabel, Kelli, Arlo…"

"Fern was delivering them." Another piece surfaced. "And Fern left her bag at the campsite when she switched with Dawn."

Callie looked up. "Her bag with her name on it."

"Right. She was moving to the trailer, figured she'd just use Dawn's bag and swap stuff later if she needed anything." I tried to picture the timeline. "So Fern's bag was sitting at her campsite, before Dawn moved in that night."

"And Dawn ended up using Fern's packets."

We looked at each other.

Callie asked carefully, "What are you thinking?"

"I'm thinking…" I hesitated, not wanting to leap to conclusions again. "I'm thinking there's a chain here. Missing samples, tampered packets, the bag switch. But I can't see the shape of it yet."

"Maybe the shape doesn't matter right now. Maybe you just need to know there's something to follow."

She was right. For the first time since yesterday's disaster, I could feel a thread—faint, but real. Not certainty or clarity—

just the sense that if I pulled carefully enough, something would unravel.

"Someone had access," I said slowly, working through it. "Someone who could take fluorite from the museum storage. Someone who helped with the gift bags. Someone who knew which bag would end up at which campsite..."

"That's a lot of someones."

"Or one very careful person." I sat back down on the bench, Des immediately pressing against my legs. "But why? That's what I can't figure out. Why go through all that trouble?"

Callie didn't answer right away; when she did, her voice was quiet. "Mom, if someone did tamper with those packets... if they put them in Fern's bag specifically..."

"Then Fern would have been the one..." I stopped myself, uneasy about saying it out loud.

"Maybe. Or maybe it's just a coincidence. Maybe Dawn was always the target and the bag switch didn't matter at all."

But the idea had lodged now, uncomfortable and insistent. Fern's bag. Fern's campsite. Fern's pink toque that Dawn had worn. All of it pointing toward someone who should have been there—but wasn't.

I didn't have proof; not even a complete theory. But the pieces were there, scattered like breadcrumbs, and for the first time since yesterday's disaster, I could feel the shape of something underneath them.

"I don't know what it means yet," I admitted.

"But you've got a thread to follow."

"Maybe." The word came out more hopeful than I'd intended.

The despair that had been crushing me since yesterday was shifting. Not into certainty—I wasn't making that mistake again—but into something steadier. Purpose, maybe. Or just the familiar rhythm of investigation—if I kept looking, kept questioning, the pattern would eventually reveal itself.

Callie stood, tucking her tablet under her arm. "Then we follow it. But first, you need food. Real food—not whatever you've been surviving on."

"I'm not hungry."

"Too bad. We're going to Mandy's after we finish closing up. You're going to have soup—and maybe some colour will come back to your face." She headed toward the counter where we'd left our coats. "Besides, if we're going to figure this out, we've got to listen. And Mandy's is where people talk."

I looked at Des, who'd returned to sit at my feet. Her tail thumped once—as if in agreement with Callie's plan.

The mystery wasn't solved. Wasn't even close. But it wasn't shapeless anymore anymore. It had edges now—possibilities. A direction to move in, even if I couldn't see where it led.

"Alright," I said, pulling on my coat. "Mandy's. But I'm buying."

"Deal. Though knowing Mandy, she'll probably feed us for free anyway."

As we locked up and headed into the October evening, I found myself thinking about patterns. About how they revealed themselves when you stopped staring too hard at one thing and let yourself see the whole picture.

I'd been so focused on Arlo and those coins that I'd missed everything happening around the edges. The museum theft. The strange flames. The gift bag left behind.

I still didn't know what it all meant—but I knew there was something there to find.

And that was enough to keep moving forward.

By the time we closed the store, the sky had deepened from bruised purple to full dark. Mandy's café glowed on the corner, yellow light spilling onto the sidewalk. Even Des perked up and tugged me toward the warmth.

Inside, the air was thick with fried onion and fresh bread scent. The usual festival energy had dimmed to something quieter—people worn down by too much news, seeking comfort in familiar booths and hot coffee. Mandy moved between tables with her trademark efficiency, sliding mugs down with the kind of brisk tenderness that dared anyone to refuse.

"Sit," she ordered the moment she spotted us, already grabbing plates.

We found a booth near the back. Des stretched across my boots with a contented sigh. Callie slumped against the vinyl seat, her tablet still clutched like a lifeline.

At the counter, Arlo and Fern waited for their take-out, paper cups steaming between them. No point in hiding now, I supposed. They hadn't noticed me yet. I could have left it there —let time and gossip do the slow work—but decency meant owning your mistakes face to face.

I stood before I could talk myself out of it. "Be right back," I told Callie.

The café quieted a little as I crossed the room. Fern's posture stiffened when she saw me. Arlo's jaw tightened, but he didn't move.

"I owe you both an apology," I said. "Not the kind that hides behind excuses. I was wrong—about all of it. I hurt you, and I made it worse by doing it in public."

Fern blinked, surprise flickering before she found her voice. "You really did," she said softly.

"I know. I can't undo it, but I can learn from it. I should have thought before I spoke. Before I judged."

Arlo exhaled, slow. "That's all any of us can do."

I nodded once, grateful he'd given me that much. "Thank you," I said, and meant it.

When I turned back toward our booth, a few people were already pretending to study their menus again. The low hum of conversation crept back in, warmer somehow. Mandy caught my eye from behind the counter and gave a small approving nod before returning to her coffee urn.

I slid into the booth beside Callie. Her hand found mine under the table, her fingers cool and steady. For the first time all day, the noise around us felt like it belonged to the town again, not to the rumour mill. Maybe this was how trust came back—not all at once, but in small, ordinary places like this.

The bell over the door jingled, and in swept Nora, Enid, and Trish, scarves flapping and cheeks pink from the night air. They spotted us immediately and made a beeline for our booth, sliding in across from us as if it had been reserved.

"Did you hear?" Nora leaned forward, eyes bright with the thrill of fresh gossip. "About Charlotte and Charlie yesterday evening?"

I braced myself for another round of speculation about Dawn's death or Arlo's coins.

"They were down by the vendor stalls," Enid jumped in. "Charlotte was in one of her moods, scolding poor Charlie about some crooked display. Sharp as a tack, that one. Told him the whole thing looked 'amateurish' and that people would judge the festival by details like that."

"But then—" Trish's voice carried that particular tone reserved for juicy revelations. "Charlie just hefted those heavy boxes like they were nothing, reset the whole thing perfectly. And Charlotte? She smiled at him."

"Not her politician's smile either," Nora added. "A real one. Proud, even. Touched his arm and said 'That's exactly right,

Charlie. I knew I could count on you.' You should have seen his face light up."

"Like a puppy getting a treat," Trish said—not unkindly. "He rearranged that booth twice more because she mentioned wanting it 'just so.' Even stayed late to make sure the lighting was perfect because she'd said something about shadows. Devotion, plain as day."

Enid nodded knowingly. "And this morning, I saw him at the community centre before dawn—double-checking all the festival displays. When I asked what he was doing up so early, he said Charlotte had mentioned she wanted everything perfect for the weekend crowds." She shook her head with fond exasperation. "That boy tracks her every word like gospel."

"Charlotte might not realize what she's doing," Nora said, "but to Charlie? A word of praise from her is like gold. That boy would walk through fire if she asked."

The phrase hung in the air. *Walk through fire.*

Their laughter bubbled up, too bright for the dim booth, but the words stayed lodged in my mind. Charlie's endless helpfulness wasn't just his nature. He was chasing those rare moments of approval, that fleeting smile. If Charlotte wanted something—anything—Charlie would see it as a mission. And if she'd even hinted that Fern's growing popularity was over-shadowing her carefully planned festival...

Mandy arrived with two plates of turkey dinner, mashed potatoes still steaming. "Eat," she ordered, setting them down firmly. "You both look like you've survived on coffee and anxiety since breakfast."

She wasn't wrong.

The Belles continued their chatter, moving on to speculation about the flames people had seen at various campsites during the festival. "Those campfire colour packets never looked quite right to me," Nora mused, shaking her head. "All those unnatural colours. Gave me the shivers."

"And that poor woman was wearing Fern's hat, wasn't she?" Enid added quietly. "Strange coincidence, that was."

Trish made a soft sound of agreement. "If you believe in coincidences."

Their voices faded into background noise as Callie nudged her tablet toward me. "Mom, look at this."

She'd been scrolling through her blog comments, but now the screen showed something different—a spreadsheet tracking patterns in the posts.

"I started sorting them properly," she said. "Most of the 'tragic accident' comments are from brand-new accounts—no history, no profile pictures. Generic usernames. But look here —" She pointed to two highlighted entries. "These two are Manitoba-based IP addresses—local."

My attention sharpened.

"And underneath all that coordinated spam, there are real comments." She scrolled down. "This one describes Dawn's campfire turning blue-white. Says the smoke smelled sharp, chemical. The person was up late reading and saw someone by the fire around eleven—wearing a pink toque. They thought it was Fern at first, but said the person seemed bigger somehow —different."

I leaned closer. That matched what I'd seen when Des and I walked past—Dawn sitting by the fire, wearing Fern's distinctive toque.

"They said the flames were the strangest colour they'd ever seen," Callie continued. "Said it looked like she'd gotten a 'bad packet' of colour flames."

The next comment snagged my attention. "That one about walking their dog past the campsite—I remember them. They told me the same thing at the gate when I was trying to keep people from leaving. Said they saw both women organizing the switch, very friendly. But that the fire later was nothing like the normal campfire colour packets everyone else was using."

The information clicked into place with what I'd been piecing together at the store. The strange flames Des had reacted to. The gift bag with Fern's name. The museum theft.

"It's exactly what you've been thinking," Callie continued. "These witnesses are backing you up. You're not imagining connections."

I looked at the comments again, reading the detailed descriptions. One person had even noted the exact time they'd seen the blue flames—around 11:30, matching the time I'd walked past with Des.

"So what are you going to do?" I asked.

Callie's expression shifted into something determined. "I'm done just deleting the spam. I'm going to document it— show people how coordinated it is. Track the patterns, expose the manipulation. And I'm going to pull these real witness accounts to the top where people can actually see them."

She looked up from the screen—and for a moment Walter's stubbornness flashed in her eyes. "This is what I was trained for, Mom. Finding the story underneath the noise. Showing people the difference between truth and manip- ulation."

Pride swelled in my chest, mixed with that familiar tug of worry. But this was her choice, her commitment to use her platform responsibly—instead of being drowned by it.

"People need to see what's really happening," she added. "Not just the version someone wants them to believe."

"Then do it," I said quietly. "Keep the truth visible."

Around us, the diner hummed with evening conversation. The Belles had moved on to debating whether the festival would continue tomorrow, their voices a comfortable backdrop. Mandy appeared with coffee refills—no asking, just pouring.

I pulled a napkin toward me and borrowed Callie's pen. Started sketching out what I knew and suspected:

1. Museum theft (fluorite missing)
2. Fern leaves her bag at campsite
3. Dawn ends up with Fern's bag
4. Fire burns strangely
5. Dawn dies

The chain was there, links visible even if I couldn't see how they connected yet. But Callie's witness comments filled in gaps—the blue-white flames, the chemical smell, the bag switch confirmed by multiple people.

I didn't know the mechanism. Couldn't prove tampering or identify who had access at the right moments. But the pattern was emerging from the fog—clearer with each piece falling into place.

Des shifted under the table, warm weight steady against my boots. Callie was absorbed in her tablet again, fingers flying as she reorganized her comment sections. The Belles' laughter rose at something Trish said—genuine and unforced.

For the first time since Jason's harsh words yesterday, the despair crushing my chest began to lift. Not into certainty—I'd learned that lesson—but into something steadier. Hope, maybe. Or just the familiar rhythm of investigation, the sense that if I kept looking, kept questioning, the pattern would eventually reveal itself completely.

Mandy appeared at our table, eyeing my half-eaten dinner with disapproval. But then she caught sight of the napkin, the list I'd been making, and her expression softened.

"You've got that look again, Tilly," she said, refilling my

coffee without a word. "Like you've nearly cracked it. Don't give up now."

I looked up at her—the woman who'd somehow become the town's steady heartbeat, who knew when people needed a slice of pie and when they needed a hard truth.

"I won't," I said, and meant it.

The smile she gave me was brief but warm. "Good. Because if anyone can figure this out, it's you."

After she left, I stared at the napkin again. The chain of events wasn't complete, but it was there—visible and real.

Callie glanced up from her work. "Feeling better?"

"Getting there." I folded the napkin carefully, tucking it into my pocket. "One step at a time."

"That's all we need." She closed her tablet with quiet satisfaction. "One step, then another, until we reach the end."

Des yawned, tail thumping once against my boot. Around us, the diner continued its evening rhythm—plates clattering, conversations rising and falling, the bell chiming as people came and went.

The mystery wasn't solved—wasn't even close—but the fog was thinning. For the first time in days, I could see far enough ahead to keep moving forward.

That would have to be enough.

CHAPTER FIFTEEN

Saturday morning arrived with the kind of pale light that made everything look a little worn at the edges. I unlocked the store door and flipped the sign to OPEN while Des sniffed her way along the baseboards, checking for changes only she could detect.

Major Crimes still hadn't arrived. Jason was running on fumes, managing everything himself while the town buzzed with half-truths and theories. The waiting had started to feel like another kind of storm building.

The coffee urn hissed as I filled it—the familiar sound settling something in my chest. Outside, the festival was waking up—someone testing a mic at the bandstand, vendors dragging equipment across gravel, the low murmur of early risers claiming breakfast spots at Mandy's. By noon tomorrow, all of it would be packed away. The thought sat heavy in my chest.

Callie appeared from the back room with the cash drawer, her tablet already balanced on one hip. "Mandy's bringing cinnamon twists later. Said we probably needed them."

"She's not wrong."

The bell jangled and Bertha stepped through, carrying a thermos and a brown paper sack that she set on the counter with her usual efficiency. "Brought sandwiches—figured you might forget to eat again."

I took the bag, noting the careful way she was watching me. "Thanks."

"Festival ends at noon tomorrow," she said, not quite a question.

"I know."

She nodded once and moved toward the coffee urn. For a moment, the store felt like it used to—ordinary, safe, the kind of place where time slowed down just enough to catch your breath.

The bell jangled again, this time admitting Nora, Trish, and Enid in a flurry of scarves and cheerful noise. They homed in on the coffee station.

"We're on our way to help Kelli set up for Brisk Morning Yoga on the Point," Nora announced, pulling three mugs from the shelf. "Charlotte was already there at sunrise, rearranging the mats like their placement would make or break the whole festival."

Trish lowered her voice to the tone reserved for particularly interesting gossip. "She mentioned they're leaving right after the festival closes. Some tourism conference in Cancún—she was very vague about details but very clear about how important it all is."

"'Wheels up,'" Enid said with obvious distaste. "Who says 'wheels up' in Balsam Bay?"

I made a note in my notebook by the register. Not because it was revelatory, just because it narrowed the window. If Charlotte and Charlie were leaving Sunday afternoon, I had less than thirty hours to figure everything out.

"Typical Bugles," Trish continued, stirring cream into her coffee. "Festival's not even over and they're already thinking about the next thing. Makes you wonder if they actually care about any of this or just the photo opportunities."

Nora patted my arm as they headed for the door. "You're looking better than you did yesterday, dear. More focused."

After they left, the store settled into its morning rhythm. A few early customers came through—tourists buying last-minute souvenirs, locals picking up coffee filters and bread. I rang them up automatically, my mind working through the same loop it had been stuck in since last night.

The bell jangled again, and Joe Charles ducked through the doorway, boots scuffing against the mat as he took in the room. He moved with that unhurried grace he had, like someone who'd learned long ago that rushing solved nothing.

"Morning," he said, nodding to Bertha and Callie before his eyes found me behind the counter.

Des was on her feet immediately, tail wagging as she crossed to greet him. He crouched down, ran his hands along her ears and neck with the kind of attention that came from years of reading dogs.

"She's settled," he said quietly, more observation than praise. "Knows her job now."

I came around the counter. "What can I get you, Joe?"

"I need rope," he said. "Heavy gauge. Got a sled harness that needs repair before winter sets in."

I led him toward the back aisle where we kept the supplies. He followed, pausing to examine a display of pocket knives on the way.

"Heard things've been rough," he said, not looking at me. "Thought I'd check in while I was here."

"Festival's been complicated," I said, which felt like the understatement of the year.

"Mm." He tested the weight of a coil of rope, then selected another. "Walter used to say you had a knack for reading the ground—could track a trail better than most."

The mention of Dad made my chest tighten. "He taught me most of what I know about that."

"He did." Joe's voice carried that quiet certainty he had. "But the instinct was yours. He just showed you how to trust it."

I pulled down the rope he'd chosen and carried it back toward the register, where Bertha was watching with interest and Callie had paused her work, tablet forgotten on the counter.

"Sometimes it's hard to see what's real and what's just noise," I said as I set the rope down.

Joe nodded slowly. "That's when you go back to basics. Look for the clearest sign. Follow that first. The rest makes sense once you know where you're headed."

Des leaned against his leg, and he scratched behind her ears without looking down, his attention still on me.

"People leave trails whether they mean to or not," he said. "You just have to notice what doesn't fit—what's shifted since yesterday."

I thought about Charlie's convenient timing, the gift bags, the missing mineral samples. Not just scattered clues anymore —movement. A path someone was trying to erase as fast as I could trace it.

"Maybe it's not about seeing the pattern," I said slowly. "Maybe it's about following where it leads."

Joe's mouth curved, approving but measured. He pulled out his wallet, counted bills onto the counter. "Then keep walking it. Just remember — sometimes the trail bites back. Trust your footing."

He tucked the rope under his arm, moved toward the door,

then paused with his hand on the frame. "Walter knew you'd figure things out when it mattered—that's why he trusted you with more than just the store."

The door closed behind him before I could ask what he meant by that.

Bertha cleared her throat. "Man doesn't waste words."

"No," I agreed. "He doesn't."

But his visit had settled something in me. The doubt that had been gnawing since yesterday's disaster with Arlo—the fear I was seeing patterns where none existed, forcing connections—eased back slightly.

I had the skills. I just needed to trust them.

With that mindset, the store felt steady under my feet—Bertha moving methodically behind the counter, Des snoring in her corner, the low hum of the coffee urn filling the quiet. Normal life, or close enough to pretend.

Callie set her tablet on the counter, angling it so I could see. "Comments are calmer this morning. Still getting the copy-paste accounts pushing 'tragic accident' and 'respect privacy,' but the real witnesses are staying visible. I'm filtering, not deleting."

"Good. Keep it that way."

She studied my face. "What are you thinking?"

"That if anything was tampered with, it happened at the gift bag assembly. That's where the path starts."

Bertha looked up from restocking the impulse rack near the register. "Who had access to those bags from start to finish?"

"Charlotte oversaw the assembly, with Charlie managing the boxes and distribution lists. Arlo dropped one load and insisted on cleaning up himself—too flustered to let anyone help. Fern worked the star chart station, while Sean had delivered the flame packets earlier in the week. Mabel and Kelli floated between tables keeping things organized. You and I had stopped in to check progress, helped for a bit, but I hadn't paid much attention to what was in each bag."

"And who showed up in places they didn't strictly need to be?" Bertha asked.

"Charlie." The name came out flat. "Always helping. Always convenient."

Callie's mouth twitched. "Helpful is definitely his brand."

I sketched a rough chain of custody on a fresh page: assembly table → labeled boxes → campground distribution → Fern's campsite → Dawn's fire. There it was, visible in arrows and block letters. Not proof, but a trail I could follow without waiting for lab results.

Des pressed against my leg, and I reached down to scratch behind her ears. The tension in my shoulders eased slightly.

"I need to re-walk the gift bag timeline," I said. "Confirm who touched what and when. If something was swapped or tampered with, there'll be a seam somewhere. People always leave seams."

"What about Sean?" Callie asked. "Didn't you say you wanted to circle back to him about his missing samples?"

"Not yet." I kept my voice casual. "If I go to Sean now and we start connecting the dots too loudly, whoever borrowed that knowledge might realize we're onto them. Better to nail down the logistics first, then bring in the science."

Bertha gave a brisk nod. "You want me on the counter while you work through this?"

"Please. And if Charlotte happens to stop by—"

"I didn't hear a word from you," Bertha finished.

"She'll probably float through at some point," I said. "She's barely touched ground all week."

Callie gathered her tablet and a stack of receipts that needed filing. "I'll keep monitoring comments and pulling any useful witness accounts to the top. Text me if you need names or email records from the committee."

I tucked my notebook into my apron pocket, the pen sliding into its familiar spot. The morning felt steadier now, the path forward clearer. Not solved. Not even close. But pointed in the right direction.

The door opened again, admitting Mrs. Kozak and her grandson. She wanted batteries and he wanted candy. I helped them both, made change, smiled when the boy thanked me with chocolate already smeared on his chin.

After they left, Callie caught my eye from across the store. "Mom?"

"Yeah?"

"You know how to do this." Not encouragement, just statement. "You always have."

Des stood when I moved toward the back room, ready to follow wherever the day led. Outside, someone laughed near the bandstand. A truck rumbled past on Main Street. The festival was still here, still moving. Noon tomorrow was coming, but it hadn't arrived yet.

I had thirty hours to prove what happened to Dawn Kessler. Thirty hours before Charlotte and Charlie could disappear behind Bugle lawyers and city distance.

It would have to be enough.

"Right," I said, mostly to myself. "Let's get to work."

By the time the store quieted again, my notebook had enough scribbles and cross-outs to qualify as evidence of obsession. I flipped back through the pages, comparing timelines, checking names against locations. The festival noise outside had become background static—something I registered but didn't truly hear.

One by one, the faces sorted themselves.

Charlotte had ambition in spades. Her uncle's niece, after all—ready with the right smile for cameras, quick to spin a story that served the Bugle interests. But the mechanics? Not her wheelhouse. She dealt in optics and messaging.

Arlo's name made me pause. I'd gone after him hard yesterday, let my frustration overrule my judgment. The coins in his pocket had felt like proof until they weren't. He'd been rattled by Dawn—distracted by his history with her, nervous about Fern finding out. None of that made him a killer. If anything, someone had used his anxiety as camouflage while they worked.

Fern. Her name on the gift bag still nagged at me, but not because I thought she'd done this. Sweet, anxious Fern— maybe the bag really had been meant for her. Maybe Dawn's death had just been terrible timing. I couldn't rule it out completely, but everything I knew about Fern pointed away from this kind of calculated violence. She wasn't the type to engineer murder—barely the type to speak up at committee meetings.

Sean gave me pause—his knowledge of minerals and their chemistry, and he provided the flame packets in the first place. For a while, that closeness had made me uneasy. He hadn't been at the lantern ceremony, which had worried me until he told me about the text—an electrical issue at the bandstand. I'd believed him. It felt more like someone had wanted him out of the way than him removing himself. He valued his reputation too much to risk being tied to something like this.

Which left Charlie.

Charlie-lifting boxes unasked, showing up wherever work

waited, smiling, helping hovering in all the right places at all the right times.

Too helpful. Too convenient. Too eager to please Charlotte, who praised him like training a dog.

I tapped my pen against the page. Joe's words came back: people leave trails whether they mean to or not. Charlie had been leaving his all week, each helpful gesture another breadcrumb I'd been too distracted to follow.

Charlotte might have had the vision and the spin, but Charlie had the access and the execution. Together they made a unit—the planning and the doing. The Bugle niece and her loyal fixer.

The bell jangled. Callie came back from delivering an order to Mrs. Henderson, her cheeks pink from the chilly air. She glanced at my notebook, then at my face.

"You've got that look," she said.

"What look?"

"The one where you've figured something out but you're not sure if you should say it yet."

I closed the notebook. "Charlie."

She set her phone on the counter. "Yeah. That makes sense."

"And Charlotte," I added, though the words felt slightly less certain as I spoke them. "He does the groundwork, she manages the story. They're a team."

Callie pulled her stool closer, arms folded on the counter. "So what's the plan?"

"I need to nail down the bag timeline. Find out exactly when Charlie had access, whether anyone saw him near Fern's bag specifically." I rubbed at my temple. "Then I take it to Jason."

"And if Jason says you don't have enough?"

"Then I find more." The resolution settled in my chest,

solid and stubborn. "Because if I don't move fast, they'll be gone by tomorrow night—out of reach and wrapped in Bugle protection."

Callie studied me, her expression between worried and pride. "You really think they did this together?"

"I think Charlie did the work and Charlotte provided the cover. Whether she knew what he was planning or just created the conditions for it…" I shook my head. "That's the part I'm not sure about yet."

Des stretched by my feet, then stood and pressed her weight against my leg. The familiar pressure steadied something in me.

"Mom." Callie's voice was quiet. "What if you're wrong again?"

The question hit harder than I expected. Yesterday's disaster with Arlo was still fresh—the public accusation, Jason's anger, Fern's humiliation. I'd been so certain then, too.

"Then I'm wrong," I said finally. "But this time I'm not making accusations in public. I'm building a case, checking the facts, and bringing it to Jason before I do anything else. No more cowboy investigating."

Callie's mouth twitched. "That's probably wise."

Bertha emerged from the back room with her coat on, keys in hand. "I'm heading out," she announced. "Gotta get things set up for the volunteer lunch." She looked us up and down as she buttoned her coat. "You two look like you're plotting again, so I'll leave you to it."

"Just trying to figure out the truth," I said.

"Well," Bertha paused at the door, "you've got a knack for that—when you're not second-guessing yourself into a pretzel. Try not to overthink it this time." She nodded once, all business. "And if you end up being wrong again, at least make it interesting."

After she left, the store felt quieter. A few tourists browsed the postcard rack, I rang up fishing lures for someone bound for the lake, but my mind kept circling back to Charlie.

Always helping. Always there. Always positioning himself exactly where he needed to be.

Callie was scrolling through her tablet, fingers moving quickly. "I've been tracking the blog comments all morning. The spam accounts pushing 'tragic accident' have gotten more aggressive. Someone's working hard to make sure this never turns into a murder investigation."

"Charlotte?"

"Or someone who reports to the Bugles." She turned the screen toward me. "Look at the timing. Every time a witness comment gets traction—someone describing the strange flames or mentioning the chemical smell—within twenty minutes there's a flood of generic 'respect the family' posts that bury it."

I studied the pattern she'd highlighted. "That takes coordination."

"And resources." Callie closed the tablet. "The Bugles have both."

Music from the bandstand carried faintly through the open door—a fiddle tune that had been playing all week. A family walked past with a bucket of donut holes and tired children, their laughter mixing with vendor calls. The festival was still alive—but I could feel Sunday coming.

I pulled my notebook closer and opened to a fresh page. Drew a timeline from Wednesday's gift bag assembly to Friday night when Dawn died. Marked every point where Charlie's name appeared.

The pattern was there. Not proof, not yet. But a shape I could follow.

Des yawned, her tail thumping once against my boot. I

reached down to scratch behind her ears, and she leaned into the touch.

Callie shifted on her stool. "So we're really doing this?"

"We're really doing this," I said. "Thirty hours until the festival ends. Until Charlie and Charlotte leave town. We use every one of them."

She nodded once, decisive. "Then we don't waste time."

I looked out the window toward Main Street. Tourists still clutching festival maps, kids with glow sticks, the cheerful machinery of community celebration grinding on despite everything. The trust that the world made sense, that tragedies were accidents rather than calculations.

"I know how this happened," I said quietly—more to myself than Callie. "Now I just need to prove who put it in motion."

Callie touched my arm, brief and reassuring. "Then let's get to work."

The notebook lay open between us, filled with names, times and connections finally starting to form a complete picture. Not finished. Not perfect. But pointed in the right direction.

Charlie had left his trail. Now I just had to follow it to the end.

The wind shifted, carrying the faint tang of bold lake air and damp leaves through the door. Beyond Main Street, the lake caught the last of the sun, a flash of copper on water that pointed straight toward the Point. For once, I knew which way to go.

CHAPTER SIXTEEN

The volunteer appreciation lunch had wrapped an hour ago, leaving the community centre looking like it had survived a very polite storm. Empty urns, half-eaten cakes, and paper plates still cluttered the folding tables. The hum of the fridge filled the pause between one task and the next.

Des sprawled beneath one, chin on her paws, half-asleep in a rectangle of sunlight beside the mop bucket.

I stacked napkins beside Mandy, who was scraping dried icing off a serving platter.

"You'd think we'd just cleaned up after a wedding."

"Wedding would've cleaned up faster." She tied off a garbage bag with a decisive snap. "At least they'd have hired help."

On my way to grab another bag from the kitchen, I caught sight of the Belles gathered in formation by the doorway—three bright cardigans, one ongoing debate. Enid held up a mixing bowl like it had personally betrayed her.

"This icing sugar's gone gritty," she declared. "Feels like someone ground up gravel."

"Probably just got damp," Nora said, leaning closer. "Still—sparkles funny, doesn't it?"

"Then toss it and wash the bowl," Trish said. "We've got three more batches waiting."

I smiled in passing—just another small kitchen crisis in a week full of them—grabbed a roll of garbage bags, and kept moving. Their argument trailed me down the hall, fading beneath the clatter of dishes and the faint sting of disinfectant.

The door swung open and Jason appeared, radio clipped to his belt, exhaustion bent into his posture.

"Major Crimes just rolled in," he said. "First unit's at the detachment. Rest are on the way."

"Finally," Mandy muttered.

"Don't count on miracles. I've got to brief them before the gossip gets there first." He gave Des a quick scratch behind the ears, dodging volunteers trying to put things to right as he headed for the exit. "Looks like you guys fed half the town."

The door swung shut behind him. I dried my hands and drifted toward the supply binder someone had left open on the counter—a guilty habit, checking details, hunting for the thing out of place. SAR training had drilled it into me: information lived in margins and footnotes, in the things people forgot to update.

I flipped through pages until I reached the entry for the campfire colour packets.

Aurora Fire Packets — Received 20 boxes / Issued 19.

The neat arithmetic left an itch between my shoulder blades.

In the margin, a note in blue ink: *Hold 1 box — VIPs / C.B.*

The handwriting had those looping letters that could belong to Charlotte—the same flourishes she used on press releases. But the ink was heavier than her usual gel pens.

"Been a busy day, hasn't it?"

Mrs. Tremaine swept the floor with the grim resolve of someone who'd seen too many bake sales. She straightened with a small groan, pressing a hand to her lower back. "Mercy, I'll feel this tomorrow. Can't imagine how many hours some folks put in, though." She gave a tired chuckle. "Saw that Charlie fellow late last night when I was coming home from the Point—lights still on in here, door half-open. Guess he doesn't know when to quit."

I glanced down at the binder again. "By any chance did you help with the gift bag assembly?"

She nodded, stepping closer to my side. "Brought the flame packets out myself. Sean sent over twenty boxes from the museum. We only counted nineteen, but with all the volunteers in and out, we figured one got misplaced." She nodded toward the page. "Looks like somebody tracked it down after all."

"Did anyone mention Charlotte setting it aside?"

Mrs. Tremaine frowned. "No. Nobody said anything about Charlotte."

She shrugged and went back to sweeping, the bristles rasping softly across the floor.

I bent over the binder again. A missing box, a late-night visit, and a neat little note that made it all look tidy. Helpful, on paper. Convenient, in practice.

Three coincidences don't happen in a town this small.

I pulled my own small notebook from my jacket pocket and wrote quickly: Reserved box – after-hours access – watch where he uses it.

I flipped the notebook closed, my mind mapping itself without permission. None of it proved anything, but the pattern whispered of intention. And intention, in my experience, was where truth began.

Des huffed again, nails clicking against the floor.

"I know," I murmured. "We've got something."

Then phones started buzzing. Not just one—half the room, all at once. Heads turned, hands reaching for pockets.

Mandy checked hers first. "Oh, my."

Callie's voice cut across the room. "What is this?"

I pulled out my own phone. The headline was clear enough:

POLICE SOURCE CONFIRMS NO FOUL PLAY IN AURORA DEATH

MAJOR CRIMES REVIEW COMPLETE—CASE CLOSED

"That's not possible. They've only just arrived."

"It's everywhere." Mandy turned her phone so we could see. The Bugle family's social-media account had already reposted it with a paragraph about transparency and relief for our beloved community.

Comments poured in beneath it—relief, gratitude, suggestions that "some people" should stop stirring up trouble where none existed.

A volunteer looked up from her phone, confusion creasing her face. "But I thought the investigation was ongoing?"

Mandy moved toward the small cluster forming near the coffee station, her voice calm and steady. "Let's not jump to conclusions based on what we read online."

Jason burst back through the door mid-call, his face tight with barely controlled fury. "No, I didn't leak anything—sir, would you just listen—yes, I know they only just got here— yes, I'll handle it." His glare swept the room before he strode back outside, the door slamming behind him.

Across the room, Callie stood frozen over her tablet, fingers moving quickly—typing, deleting, typing again.

"They're tagging me. Saying I made everything up for clicks."

"Don't answer," I said, moving toward her.

"I already did!" Her tablet pinged. She looked at the screen and went pale.

Account flagged for review. Posting suspended pending investigation.

"They shut me down." Her voice came out flat.

Mandy reached over, grip firm on her shoulder. "Step back, sweetheart. They're burying you in noise. That's all this is."

Callie's jaw set, eyes bright with tears she wouldn't let fall. "If I'd kept quiet, none of this would've happened." She grabbed her bag and bolted for the door, nearly colliding with a volunteer carrying a box of leftover programs.

The words hit harder than they should have. For a second, I saw Arlo's shocked face again, the crowd gathering around us, the heat of my own certainty that had turned out to be wrongness.

Around me, volunteers murmured over their phones, thumbs scrolling, the false headline already settling into accepted truth. The fragile sense of momentum I'd built since yesterday morning cracked like ice under sudden weight.

My chest tightened, fingers going cold. The old reflex kicked in—the one that said when things went wrong, it was because I'd pushed too hard, asked too many questions, refused to leave well enough alone.

Des huffed again, nails clicking against the floor.

"I know," I murmured.

I looked back at the binder. Aurora Point kept surfacing— same names, same box. If Charlie was headed there tonight, I needed to see it myself.

I pulled out my notebook, wrote Aurora Point — tonight, and slipped it in my pocket. The forged note, the after-hours visit, that missing box—none of it had changed. The smoke-screen was just smoke.

Outside, the wind picked up—like the story wasn't finished with us yet.

———

By late afternoon, the panic had thinned. The festival grounds felt quieter now, music drifting faint from the square. Lantern strings blinked on one by one, spilling gold across the street.

I watched Callie pace beside the car, phone pressed to her ear. Callie's voice had gone brittle.

"Yeah, I've already filed an appeal. Yes, I know it's automated. Okay. Thanks."

She ended the call, stared at the dark screen for a long beat, then tucked the phone into her bag.

"I need to go home," she said. "Get screenshots before they vanish."

"Let it breathe for a night."

Callie gave a short laugh. "The algorithm's already decided I'm a liar. If I don't act fast, everything I built disappears."

"You don't have to fight this alone."

"If I don't, who's going to?" Her voice cracked. "They're saying I used Grandpa's memorial for clicks. I can't let that stand."

I reached out, but she stepped back. "I just need to fix this. You get that, right?"

"I get it."

She hesitated. "Just... don't make this worse for yourself, okay?"

"I can handle it."

"That's what worries me."

She gave a fragile half-smile and slid into the driver's seat. The taillights blinked red, then merged with traffic. When the car disappeared, the space felt emptier.

Des circled once at my feet, then sat facing the road, ears up.

"All right, girl. Looks like it's just us again."

I opened the truck door and pulled out my canvas pack—flashlight, notebook, spare charger, granola bar. The same kit I'd carried through a hundred searches and too many nights.

From somewhere behind the community centre came the thump of doors and the scrape of boxes. I followed the sound.

Charlie was stacking boxes into his pickup, humming something cheerful. One smaller box sat off to the side, half-buried under extension cords.

Aurora Fire Packets — RESERV.

The lettering was neat but overworked—those same looping strokes, ink darker than it needed to be.

I stepped closer, boots crunching gravel.

Charlie straightened and turned. "Well, if it isn't our town's favourite sleuth."

"Long day?"

"Long week." He wiped his palms on his jeans. "Charlotte wants the last of these up at the Point. VIP kits. You know how she is."

"Running them up yourself?"

"Someone's gotta." He smiled. "Can't trust the kids not to drop the fancy stuff."

I glanced at the boxes. "VIP kits. Sounds fancy."

"You'd be amazed what folks'll pay for a view and a photo under the lights."

"Exposure," I said.

He laughed. "Relax, Tilly. Not everything's a conspiracy."

"No. Some things repeat until you notice them."

His grin flickered before he looked away.

"Generous of you," I added.

He chuckled. "Hey, anything for the festival."

The air between us was polite on the surface, but colder currents moved underneath.

Des stood behind me—silent, still. A low growl would've been less unsettling than that watchful quiet.

I nodded toward the boxes. "Need a hand?"

"Nah." He slid the last box into place and pushed the tailgate closed. "All good. You heading up tonight?"

"Thinking about it."

"Then I'll see you there." He gave a two-finger salute, climbed into the driver's seat, and pulled away.

Gravel spat under his tires, the sound fading into the trees.

I watched until the truck vanished around the bend. The handwriting on that box stayed with me—those looping letters, the lines a shade too careful, the ink heavier than it should've been. I'd learned to trust that gut-tightening before a storm—the same warning hum now, low and certain.

I breathed out slowly. Jason was still at the detachment, buried in fallout. Callie was driving into her own storm. And Charlie was heading to the one place designed to pull every eye skyward.

I turned to Des. "You ready?"

The shepherd rose, tail low but steady. Her eyes locked on mine, waiting.

"Thought so."

I climbed into my SUV, started the engine, and pulled onto the narrow road out of town. The headlights swept over empty vendor booths and abandoned flyers. Beyond them, the horizon glowed faint green.

The road unwound through the trees like a ribbon caught in wind. Here and there, flashes of light caught on wet leaves, turning them to silver. People got lost chasing pretty things—sky, money, praise. Maybe that's why Dad always said to keep one foot on solid ground.

The engine hummed steady beneath my hand, familiar as breath. Somewhere ahead, the first murmurs of laughter and socializing from Aurora Point drifted down the hill. It was starting already.

I shut off the radio and cracked the window. Cool air poured in, sharp with pine and the first hint of frost. I let the silence stretch.

My phone pinged: *Kp 5 – Strong Activity Expected.*

Of course. Everyone would be watching the sky tonight. Perfect night for someone who didn't want eyes on the ground.

I glanced at Des, whose ears twitched toward the windshield. "Let's go see what our helpful friend's up to."

We crested the ridge. Above the trees, green and violet curtains trembled against the dark.

I tightened my grip on the wheel. Des's tail thumped once. The sky flickered again, green spilling like paint across black water.

CHAPTER SEVENTEEN

The parking area at Aurora Point was busy—red-filtered flashlights cut through the dark, boots crunched on gravel, lanterns rocked in the wind. It was nearly eight forty-five, and the aurora forecast was about to earn its keep.

Des padded beside me, steady and quiet. Her ears swivelled toward the trailhead where voices carried in the cold air—Charlotte's among them.

By the time I reached the rope gate, a volunteer stood behind a folding table with a clipboard and lantern, its glow painting frost onto his sleeves. Charlotte faced him across the gap, her smile bright and immovable.

"These are donors," she was saying. "They've come a long way to be here tonight. I'm sure you can make an exception."

The volunteer flipped through his checklist. "We're at capacity until the next rotation, ma'am. The point holds fifty people safely—we have to stay within the limit."

Behind Charlotte, her group milled about—twelve, maybe fifteen people in wool coats and expensive down jackets. And Charlie, standing slightly apart, hefting a supply box with extension cords coiled on top and paper bags of snacks.

On top sat the small carton: *Aurora Fire Packets — RESERV.*

Those same over-careful letters, ink too dark. The sight hit me with that low warning hum.

Charlotte tilted her chin. "Do you really want to be the one who tells the mayor's niece that her guests can't attend a festival event she helped organize?"

The volunteer's shoulders sagged. He set down his clip-board and lifted the rope.

"Fine, but only your group—and stay within the marked zone at the top. We'll reopen the trail at nine-thirty for the next rotation."

"Perfect." Charlotte waved her people through. "Come on, everyone. Single file, please."

The group filed past in twos and threes, their voices bright with anticipation. Charlie brought up the rear, box balanced carefully in his arms, head down like he was concentrating on not dropping anything. The glow from nearby lanterns caught his profile for half a second—that familiar helpful expression, eager and unassuming—before he turned uphill and disap-peared among the trees.

When the rope dropped back into place, the volunteer turned to me. "Sorry, Ms. Lafleur. Next slot's nine-thirty. We're already over the load on the point as it is."

Behind me, grumbling started low, then swelled.

"Always the same. VIPs first."

"Guess money buys a better view of public land."

A woman I didn't recognize shook her head. "We've been waiting since eight."

I could've argued. Could've flashed a smile and claimed media credentials through Callie's blog. But drawing attention would have meant alerting Charlotte—or worse, Charlie. So I stepped back, pretending patience while my pulse drummed against my ribs.

Des sat beside my boot, ears flicking toward the dark ridge above. She'd picked up on my tension, the way dogs do.

"We'll wait," I murmured, more to myself than to her.

She gave a small huff that sounded like reluctant agreement.

Lantern light shifted over the gravel as the volunteers reset the gate and checked their rotation schedules. The crowd around me thickened—maybe twenty people now, restless but resigned to the bureaucracy of small-town event management. Someone passed around paper cups of cocoa from a thermos, the steam rising in pale wisps. A volunteer near the kiosk checked his radio, muttering something about "load limits" and "rotation delays" to his partner. The night had the feel of something running just slightly out of rhythm, like music played a half-beat too slow.

I pulled out my phone and typed: *Following Charlie to Point. Charlotte + VIPs already ahead.*

No signal. The base of the point had always been a dead zone. I pocketed the phone and stared at the tree line where Charlie's flashlight had vanished.

The minutes stretched. Nine o'clock came and went. Laughter drifted from up the trail—Charlotte's voice bright and assured. The rest of us shifted in place, stamping our feet against the cold, trading small talk about the forecast.

"Supposed to peak tonight," someone said.

"Already saw violet over the lake on the drive up."

All I could think about was Charlie's box and how far ahead he was getting—with whatever he was carrying.

Around nine-twenty, the volunteer glanced at his watch, then at his radio. Still no reply from the wardens on the point. Finally he sighed and lifted the rope.

"Alright—go ahead. We'll have to sort numbers at the top. Please stay together on the trail and watch your footing."

Relief rippled through the waiting crowd. I nodded to Des and she tucked into a heel on my left.

"Busy night?" I asked the volunteer as we passed.

He smiled wearily, his face lined with exhaustion. "Something changed after supper. Word got out the lights were strong tonight—Kp-index hitting five, maybe six. Everyone wants their last look before the festival ends tomorrow." He gestured vaguely toward the ridge. "We've never had this many people up here at once."

Something had changed. The energy, the noise, even the air felt swollen with too many people chasing the same patch of sky. What should have been a peaceful evening under the stars had turned into something else—crowded, chaotic, unpredictable.

We joined the slow line of lanterns moving up the path. The trail switchbacked through birch and spruce, narrow and uneven. Twenty minutes at a steady pace, but the rhythm of boots and breath closed in around us.

Des walked close to my side. Every few steps she'd glance up at me, checking I was still focused.

When we reached the first overlook, the horizon had cracked open with a faint green shimmer. A few people stopped to point. Someone gasped.

Des pressed against my leg.

"Almost there, girl," I whispered.

The volunteer at the rear of our group called up the trail, "Nine-thirty rotation, all accounted for!"

Lanterns bobbed ahead like scattered stars, marking the route through the trees. My pulse matched their sway—anticipation threaded with something sharper, more urgent. I wasn't chasing the lights tonight. I was chasing the truth that had gone up this trail ahead of me, carried in a supply box by someone who thought helpfulness was the perfect disguise.

The path curved one last time, the incline flattening as the trees thinned. Voices drifted down from above—laughter, exclamations, the sound of a crowd already gathered.

By the time we reached the point, the lights were already in motion.

Aurora Point spread before us—wide granite jutting out over Echo Lake. Tonight it wasn't the peaceful viewing platform I remembered.

Clusters of people dotted the outcrop. Families with folding chairs. Photographers hunched over tripods. Lanterns glowed orange against the stone. Wardens moved through the crowd with radios and uneasy smiles. Someone stretched a rope line along the lip of the Point.

The aurora forecast had pulled what felt like half the province out here, and Charlotte's VIP group had tipped it past capacity. The crowd pressed toward the rope, boots scraping granite, breath pluming silver. I'd barely stepped onto the exposed rock before I realized we weren't just visitors anymore. We were just more weight on stone already groaning.

Des leaned lightly against my leg, steady as always, nose lifted to the cold air. Her ears swivelled, following movements I couldn't see.

I skirted a knot of photographers to find space near the rope line. From here I could see the lake shimmer below, already catching hints of green from the aurora building overhead.

A warden's radio crackled nearby: "Load limit's at maximum. We'll hold the trail rotation until further notice."

Des settled at my feet. I scanned the crowd for Charlie. Found Charlotte instead, standing with donors near the cocoa station—playing tour guide.

But no sign of Charlie yet.

"You made it."

I turned. Sean stood a few feet away, thermos in hand, tired lines at the corners of his eyes.

"Long hike?"

"Longer wait. Charlotte's VIPs got priority access."

"Sounds about right." He offered the thermos. "Coffee—or something pretending to be."

I took a sip—lukewarm, but welcome. "You look like you've got something on your mind."

He glanced around before lowering his voice. "Jason asked me to run that ash sample from Dawn's campfire—before Major Crimes showed up."

My pulse stuttered. "And?"

"Fluorite traces—that explains the blue-white flames you saw."

"Didn't one of your fluorite samples go missing at the museum?"

Sean's eyebrow lifted, but he didn't answer. His gaze drifted out toward the lake. The silence stretched just long enough to be deliberate.

I tucked it away carefully, the way you mark a trail you know you'll need to find again.

Around us, the murmur of voices swelled and receded like the tide. Children pointed at the strengthening lights. Someone laughed too loudly. A warden moved past with his radio pressed to his ear, speaking in low, clipped tones about capacity and rotation schedules.

The crowd pressed closer to the rope line, everyone angling for the best view, the perfect photo. The granite shelf felt smaller with every passing minute, the space contracting as more people shifted and jostled for position.

Des's ears flicked forward suddenly. I followed her gaze.

Across the outcrop, near the refreshment table, Charlie had appeared. His arms were full of gear, and there on top—the small carton.

Aurora Fire Packets — RESERV.

The same over-polished loops, ink too dark. Recognition hit hard.

Charlie set down the carton and flipped open the box. The packets inside glinted under lantern light—the box looked almost full, just a couple missing from the top.

He raised his voice above the crowd. "Extras for the VIPs! Take a few—keep the magic going at your campsites!"

A few people laughed. Charlie grinned, pressing packets into outstretched hands, urging people to take more. He tilted the box toward a well-dressed couple.

His movements were brisk—too brisk. The box rattled softly. There was urgency underneath the cheerfulness that didn't match the casual atmosphere.

To anyone else, it probably looked generous. To me, it looked like a man trying to make something disappear.

"Did you see that?" I murmured.

Sean followed my gaze. "Looks like he's just—"

I cut him off. "Helping," I finished. "He's always helping."

The crowd shifted, drawn by Charlie's cheerfulness. Overhead, the aurora brightened—green veils rippling from horizon to zenith, shot through with violet and blue. The whole gathering gasped. Cameras clicked like insects.

Then Charlotte's voice cut through. "Where did you get those?"

The chatter died. Heads turned.

Charlotte stood ten metres away, framed by aurora glow, her expression caught between confusion and something harder to read.

"I thought we used every packet during assembly."

The crowd around Charlie went quiet.

His smile faltered for half a beat before he caught it. "You told me to hold one box for the VIPs, remember? You signed off yourself. In the binder."

For a heartbeat, Charlotte's face went blank. Genuine confusion flickered across her features—as if she was searching her memory and coming up empty.

Then pride snapped her spine straight.

"Yes, of course." Her chin lifted. "For donors. I can't recall every small detail in the middle of festival chaos, but yes. That sounds right."

She turned away quickly, pivoting toward her VIP group with a forced laugh. "The lights are really picking up now, aren't they? This is exactly what we hoped for!"

To the crowd, the moment passed like a brief misstep. People turned back to the sky, to the spectacle overhead.

But I'd seen it. That flicker of doubt—the instant she realized she'd just covered for something she didn't understand. She'd covered for him—and didn't even know why.

Sean exhaled. "Well, that was awkward."

I didn't answer. My focus stayed on Charlie, wiping his hands on his jeans—small, quick movements. The box sat at his feet, nearly empty. He glanced once toward Charlotte—seeking confirmation, gratitude, some sign she'd meant to back him up.

All he got was her turned shoulder.

Something crossed his face then—disappointment, maybe, or the realization he was alone in whatever he'd done. Then he straightened, pasted his grin back in place, and carried the carton toward the far edge of the Point.

The aurora flared brighter—massive curtains folding over violet and blue, the whole sky alive. The lake below gleamed like liquid glass. Gasps rippled through the crowd—then only light and colour.

But my eyes stayed on the ground—on the man walking away with an almost-empty box and a story that didn't hold together.

Des pressed against my leg, muscles taut beneath her fur.

Sean shifted his weight. "Tilly—"

"He brought it up here," I said quietly. "Carried his guilt right out into the open."

"What are you going to do?"

I didn't have an answer. Not yet.

Overhead, the aurora danced, indifferent to the dramas below. The crowd stood rapt, faces tilted skyward, everyone chasing beauty and wonder.

Everyone—but me.

CHAPTER EIGHTEEN

Sunday morning arrived in a wash of pale light that made everything look a little worn around the edges. I'd made it home from Aurora Point after midnight, but sleep hadn't come easily. Every time I closed my eyes, I saw Charlie's grin—the small box balanced on the crate, Charlotte's confusion hanging in the air.

By the time the sun came up, the aurora had faded, but the unease hadn't.

October had settled in for good. The birches behind the community centre glowed pale gold; the maples had begun to let go—red leaves drifted across the gravel in lazy spirals. The air carried that faint metallic edge that hints at snow.

The grounds were half taken apart already. Canopies slumped like tired shoulders, cords coiled at their feet. Des trotted beside me, ears forward, tail low, nose buried in the drift of leaves.

"Mom!"

Callie crouched near the main doors of the community centre, camera angled over a paper lantern half-buried in wet leaves. Her ponytail listed to one side, shadows pooled under her eyes, but her hands stayed steady.

"You look like you haven't slept."

"Occupational hazard. You?"

"Better. I stayed up writing a statement—just facts, no drama. Sent it to sponsors and the festival committee. My account's still suspended, but the library shared it for me." She managed a small smile. "Fewer knives out this morning."

"That's good."

"If they remember the lights and not the gossip, I can live with that."

A volunteer passed us carrying a stack of folding chairs, nodding a tired greeting. Through the open doors, I could hear the scrape of tables being dragged across the floor, someone's laughter echoing off the high ceiling. The festival dismantled itself with the same brisk efficiency that had built it.

Inside, volunteers stacked chairs with the slow movements of people who'd made it through. Someone swept confetti while humming off-key. Des padded across the floor, investigated a paper bag near the refreshment table, then returned to my side.

Sean appeared by the coffee urn, rubbing his face as though trying to wake a different day. His jacket was rumpled, stubble showing more grey than I remembered. He looked like he'd been up as long as I had.

"Morning."

"Barely."

He handed me a folded printout, paper still warm from the printer. "Ran the ash sample again overnight. Same result."

I scanned the columns of data. "Fluorite traces."

"Enough to explain the blue-white flames. Major Crimes have been on the campsite since yesterday. Jason's stuck playing local liaison."

"Appreciate the warning."

He managed a tired half-smile and started for the exit. At the door he paused. "Figured you'd move faster than the red tape... if you're following any threads."

Callie watched him go. "He looks like he's fuelled by caffeine and spite."

"So's everyone else," I said.

A woman I vaguely recognized from the gift bag assembly waved as she passed, arms full of leftover promotional materials. "Quite a weekend," she said cheerfully.

"Quite a weekend," I agreed.

We followed the back corridor past the kitchen. The hallway narrowed, boxes leaning against walls. Des's claws clicked softly on tile.

At the far end, luggage sat stacked beside the office door— two hard-shell cases in charcoal grey, a garment bag, and a canvas tote with an airline tag.

Callie stepped closer, reading the tag. "Cancún. Leaving tonight."

Charlotte's voice reached us from the next room before she emerged—sleek black boots, latte in one hand, phone pressed to her ear. Sunglasses perched on her head despite the grey morning.

"—yes, confirm the car for two. Perfect." She ended the call and aimed a bright smile our way. "Good morning! Didn't expect so many here so early."

"Lots to do before the festival wraps up."

"How organized of you." She gestured toward the luggage. "Charlie and I are flying out right after. Tourism conference in Cancún—all networking and no sunshine, unfortunately."

"Sounds urgent," Callie said.

"These things always are." Charlotte was already scrolling

her phone, half-turned toward the exit. "The festival was a triumph despite... well, despite everything."

I stepped closer to the table, where the open binder sat under a pile of flyers. "Before you go—quick question about the supply log."

She paused mid-scroll. "The what?"

"The Aurora Fire packets. There's a note in the margin—*Hold 1 box, VIPs, C.B.* That's your handwriting, right?"

Charlotte's expression went blank for half a beat, like someone searching a filing cabinet and coming up empty. Then her chin lifted. "I can't be expected to narrate every scribble in a festival binder during that kind of chaos. If you've got detailed questions about boxes and paperwork, ask Charlie—he lives for that kind of thing."

She was already moving down the hall, boots clicking.

Callie exhaled. "That was—"

"Vanity," I finished. "She doesn't remember writing it because she didn't. But admitting she doesn't know would make her look disorganized."

We ducked into the small admin nook where supply binders sat stacked on a folding table. I flipped mine open.

Aurora Fire Packets — Received 20 boxes / Issued 19.

Beside that, in neat blue ink: *Hold 1 box — VIPs / C.B.*

"Those are Charlotte's initials," Callie said.

"Written by Charlie." I traced the looping letters, feeling the slight indentation where the pen had pressed too hard. "Same hand as the *RESERV* label. Same over-polished loops, same heavy pressure. He forged both."

"You're sure?"

"Mrs. Tremaine saw him in here after hours. Next morning, this note appears. Perfect shield—Charlotte's initials, Charlotte's authority. If anyone questioned the reserved box, she'd instinctively defend it."

"Which she just did."

"Exactly."

I flipped to my notes. The supply log. The *RESERV* carton. Mrs. Tremaine's sighting. Charlie at the Point, offloading packets with that helpful energy. Dad's memorial—Charlie coordinating, Charlie tidying, Charlie always exactly where he needed to be.

"He inserts himself whenever things get complicated," I said. "Makes himself indispensable. Then when questions come later, he's already cleaned up the evidence and created a paper trail that points anywhere but at him."

Callie's jaw tightened. "So once they're on that plane, it's over."

"Out of reach—wrapped in lawyers and a tourism-conference alibi. By the time Major Crimes processes their samples, Charlie and Charlotte will be back from Cancún with synchronized stories."

"So we move now."

"We move now. But carefully." I glanced toward the back of the building where Charlie's humming drifted from somewhere deeper in. "We're helping with inventory, putting things away, making conversation. Smile. Ask questions. Let him think we're wrapping loose ends."

"You're better at smiling than I am."

"Then I'll lead. You observe. Take notes if you need to—journalist instinct and all."

She nodded, some of the tension leaving her shoulders. Having a role helped. Having a purpose.

We stepped back into the main hall just as a gust sent red leaves skating across the parking lot. Through the tall windows, a gust scattered red leaves across the parking lot. Volunteers moved between tables with easy rhythm. Two women laughed over tangled string lights.

"Everything's so calm again," Callie said, as if the air itself didn't remember last night.

"Note it for your wrap post."

At the mouth of the corridor leading toward the back, I paused.

Des pressed against my leg, ears forward, a quiet tremor running through her flank.

"You ready?" I asked Callie.

She tightened her ponytail. "Ready."

———

Morning light cut through the open double doors that led to the parking lot, catching on the clutter of boxes and half-empty cartons. The air was cool and faintly stale, the kind of stillness that follows too much activity.

Charlie stood at a folding table near the doors, humming while he sorted supplies. Extension cords coiled in perfect loops. Clipboards fanned in a neat arc. Everything looked finished. Efficient. Benign.

"Morning!" he called. "Here to help close things out?"

"Thought we'd lend a hand."

Callie lifted her camera an inch. "Documentation for the wrap post."

Des settled just inside the doors, one eye on us, one on the parking lot.

Charlotte appeared in the doorway, phone pressed to her ear, voice bright with control. "Yes, flying in from Winnipeg. Perfect, thank you." She glanced at her watch.

Charlie flicked tape off his fingers. "Big day. Almost wrapped."

"Almost," I agreed.

We kept it warm. Kept it ordinary. He was winning by pretending everything was normal, and both of us knew it.

"I wanted to ask about last night. That small box marked *RESERV*."

"All used up." His response came smooth, eyes still on his stacks. "VIP packets, distributed at the Point. Charlotte had it noted in the binder—C.B., right?" He glanced toward her with an easy smile.

Charlotte, still on her call, gave a vague nod without looking. "VIP fast track arrival, yes."

"Efficient system."

"Someone's got to keep track." The humming returned.

I let a beat pass. "And my father's memorial. Those coins turning up scattered like that—funny how they ended up pointing in all the wrong directions."

His chuckle came quick and brittle, meant to dismiss. "Still chasing that, Tilly? Whole lot of drama over an old man's keepsakes." He straightened edges that were already straight. "Sometimes things just get messy. Doesn't mean there's a story."

Outside, wind caught a tent someone was folding. A volunteer yelped, another laughed, and together they wrestled the canvas flat. Inside, Charlie's tape gun made a clean rip as he sealed another box.

He gestured to the space around him—the labeled stacks, the swept floor. "The police inspectors already came through yesterday. Logged everything, photographed what they needed." His expression softened. "You don't have to keep carrying this weight."

Beside me, Callie's voice fell to a whisper. "Maybe he's right."

For a moment, the room felt off-balance. Boxes squared to corners. Labels crisp. Air too still. A helpful man humming while he worked, flight ticking closer with every folded tarp outside.

Then light caught the edge of a carton stacked half-behind the table. A faint green smear traced the seam where the tape had been replaced. The label—fresh ink still glossy, hand-writing looped and over-careful.

I shifted two steps. "Mind if I angle this box? Light's better here for Callie's photos."

"Let me—" He was there in an instant, smile fixed, movements practiced and quick. "Those edges catch if you're not careful."

"They do." I held my position, let morning sun find that greenish dust along the seam.

Something flickered across his face—shorter than surprise, flatter than fear. He wiped the edge with his sleeve and laughed, soft and breathy. "Cardboard picks up everything in a place like this." His tone was light, but the sleeve he'd used stayed angled away from the sun.

"Sometimes it keeps things, too."

He set the box back, perfectly aligned, then turned to face me with that boyish grin. "What are you really trying to say, Tilly?"

"Just that patterns repeat. Sometimes they say more than words do."

His grin thinned. When he spoke, his tone stayed friendly but something underneath had shifted. "Careful. Keep pushing and Charlotte takes the fall. That the kind of drama you're trying to stir up?"

Something behind the words changed the temperature of the room—less a threat, more a quiet reminder of how things worked here. How names like Bugle didn't have to be spoken to fill a space. He said "Charlotte," but what I heard was the family name behind her. The power that bankrolled this festival, controlled the town council, owned the locks on half the doors we all pretended were public.

Callie's camera strap creaked in her grip. I felt her stillness beside me.

I kept my expression neutral. "You seem to know where all the lines are."

"Let's just say I know who signs the cheques around here."

Charlotte looked up from her phone, startled. "Charlie?" The question small, uncertain. Then, too brightly, "Anyway, the car will be here soon. We should finish up."

Charlie reached for his suitcase and tipped it upright. The wheels hit concrete with a hollow thump. He angled toward the open doors.

He'd already shifted his weight before the suitcase moved. I took one small step and was simply there—not blocking, not making a scene. Just in his path, shoulder square, gaze steady.

"Running's an answer. Don't make it yours."

He stopped close enough that I could see the small cut on his knuckle where tape had caught him. For a heartbeat we only listened—the wind moving through the open doors, the flap of a stray tarp outside.

Charlotte watched from near the interior doorway, caught between loyalty and confusion.

"If you're worried about Charlotte," I said, voice low enough that only he could hear, "stop using her as your shield."

Colour rose, then drained, moving under his skin. He took a slow breath, held it, let it go.

Outside, the tent crew's laughter rose as they got the canvas to fold properly. Light shifted another degree across the asphalt. Inside, truth balanced on a knife edge.

I held his gaze. He held mine.

Des shifted near the doorway, a soft whine barely audible.

Charlie's smile returned, thinner now, edges tight. "Always so dramatic, Tilly." He glanced at Charlotte. "We should go. Don't want to miss the flight."

Charlotte moved to his side automatically. Together they walked toward the open doors, rolling case between them, stepping out into the bright morning.

From where I stood, they still looked united. A team.

Callie exhaled slowly. "We almost had him."

"No," I said, watching them disappear into the parking lot. "We still have him."

Des padded over and pressed against my leg. Outside, an engine slowed, gravel crunching as a car rolled to a stop.

"What now?" Callie asked.

I crouched near the box Charlie had been organizing, the one with the faint green smear along the seam. Under the hum of fluorescent lights, the dust glimmered like ground glass. I touched it—gritty, heavier than cardboard residue.

The same texture Enid had mentioned yesterday—that gritty "icing sugar."

My stomach dropped.

"The kitchen," I said, straightening. "Right now."

We found the Belles exactly where I'd hoped—still tidying Charlotte's makeshift office and the kitchen prep area, moving with the brisk determination of women who couldn't leave a mess behind even if the building caught fire.

"Don't wash that bowl yet," I called as we pushed through the doorway.

All three turned. Enid stood at the sink, hands halfway submerged in suds, a mixing bowl balanced on the edge.

"This one?" she asked, frowning. "I was just about to—"

"Let me see it first."

She passed it over. Under the bright overhead lights, I saw

what Nora had noticed yesterday—a faint shimmer clinging to the rim and base, pale green dust that refused to rinse away.

"That's not icing sugar," I said quietly.

Nora leaned in, squinting through her glasses. "I used to make my own ceramic glazes. That's mineral dust. See how it catches the light?"

"Someone used this bowl to grind something," Trish added. "Look at the scratches on the bottom."

I set the bowl on the counter and crouched to open the cabinet beneath the sink. "Help me look. Anything that doesn't belong."

The Belles dove in with the enthusiasm of women who'd been waiting all week for a proper mystery. Spray bottles clattered aside. Dishcloths piled up. Enid unearthed an old cutting board; Nora found a bent whisk.

Then Trish straightened. "What's this?"

She held a cracked ceramic mortar, the pestle snapped clean in half. The grinding surface shimmered faintly green.

"Museum piece," Nora murmured, tugging a folded tag from underneath. She smoothed it open. "Says so right here."

I took the tag, my pulse kicking hard.

Fluorite Sample #27 — Museum Collection

Sean's handwriting. Neat, precise, unmistakable.

Enid let out a low whistle. "Whoa. Someone ground up a museum sample in our kitchen?"

"Not just someone." I photographed the tag, the mortar, the bowl. "Charlie. After hours, when no one was here to see."

Callie stared at the evidence spread across the counter. "He tried to hide it under the sink."

"And almost got away with it." I slipped the tag into my pocket, careful not to smudge the ink. "But he couldn't erase everything."

Nora crossed her arms, expression hardening. "That boy's been helpful all week. Too helpful."

"Always first to volunteer," Trish said. "Always around when the trash went out."

"Because he was covering his tracks," I said.

Des's nails clicked softly on the linoleum as she stepped closer, ears forward, tail still.

Enid wiped her hands on her apron, mouth set. "What do you need from us?"

"Nothing else," I said. "You three just closed the case."

I pulled out my phone—full signal bars standing near the kitchen window. The text I'd tried to send Jason last night still sat unsent in my outbox. I hit Send.

The Belles exchanged glances—sharp, satisfied, the look of women who'd just proven they were more than background chatter.

"Go get him, Tilly," Nora said, voice full of mischief and satisfaction.

I intended to.

CHAPTER NINETEEN

We stepped into the morning air—sharp and clean after the musty cupboards inside. The parking lot behind the community centre stretched before us, nearly empty now. Damp bunting and flattened streamers clung stubbornly to the asphalt. The last food vendor was packing up across the square, burnt sugar mixing with the scent of October leaves.

Festival music had faded, leaving only the scrape of folding chairs and volunteers calling to one another. Across the lot, I caught a glimpse of something I hadn't expected—CLAIM and LANTERN volunteers folding the same tent, trading easy jokes as they worked. The sight should've felt impossible after everything, but it just looked like any other Sunday morning.

Charlotte stood by a silver sedan, phone to her ear, issuing directions in that brisk committee voice. Beside her, Charlie eased the last piece of luggage—a garment bag—into the trunk beside its matching suitcases.

Des lay at my feet, tail sweeping slow arcs through the

gravel dust. The autumn sun was sharp enough to make me squint.

"Mom," Callie said quietly beside me. "They're about to leave."

I stepped forward, keeping my voice level, polite. "Before you head out, I need to clear up something from the inventory."

Charlie turned, that easy grin snapping into place. "Always happy to help."

"The binder note," I said. "The one that appeared after Mrs. Tremaine saw you in here late Friday night—*Hold 1 box — VIPs / C.B.* Same looping handwriting and heavy ink as the *RESERV* label."

His smile flickered, then steadied. "Charlotte wanted extras set aside for donors. I just followed orders."

Charlotte's phone lowered. "I never said that."

The quiet hit harder than shouting ever could. Even the gulls over the lake seemed to still.

I took another step, closing the distance until he had to meet my eyes.

"Then maybe explain why that same handwriting shows up on the *RESERV* box—the one you brought to Aurora Point.

And why the same pale-green smear showed up in the ash Major Crimes collected from Dawn's campfire."

From my pocket, I drew the crumpled museum tag and held it up so the sunlight caught the faint green dust still clinging to it.

"Sean's fluorite sample," I said, keeping my voice low and even. "The one you ground into powder in the community centre kitchen. The one you tried to hide under the sink."

The change was instant—his posture stiffened, that easy mask cracking. His eyes fixed on the tag, recognition flooding his face before he could stop it.

He didn't answer. His hands balled into fists, knuckles white.

"You were in here after hours," I said. "You forged Charlotte's initials to make it look like she'd set a box aside. You handed out the packets yourself—just enough to make it seem nothing was missing. But one was different. You tampered with it."

His throat worked. "I didn't—"

Charlotte looked at him then, disbelief cutting sharp. That single look shattered him faster than anything I could've said.

"It wasn't my idea," he said at last, voice rough. "The memorial—someone higher up wanted to stir things up. I was told to make sure it went off without a hitch. Then, during the service, they saw the display box—thought it might help their message. Asked if I could handle it."

He gave a short, broken laugh. My stomach turned. "Said it'd be a good test."

There were only a few people in town who could make an order sound like praise.

"I did what I was told. Took the box, passed it over, got it back later. Then they told me to leave it where it'd be found. Said I'd done good work."

Charlotte's face went pale. "Oh, Charlie..."

She pressed a hand to her chest.

The wind gusted, rattling loose metal somewhere behind the building. Des shifted beside me, ears forward.

"You tampered with the Aurora Fire packet meant for Fern," I said, the words tasting like metal.

He nodded once, hollow. "I did. Ground up some of Sean's minerals—thought it would be just enough to make her feel off for a day or two. I figured if she was laid up, she couldn't steal the spotlight."

His hands trembled as he spoke. "I never meant for anyone to get hurt."

I swallowed hard. "But Fern never used it."

"No." His voice barely rose above the wind. "The podcaster grabbed it instead."

Charlotte's breath caught—somewhere between a gasp and a sob.

"No one told you to do that," she said.

"No. That was me." His eyes found hers. "I just wanted to make you proud. Make every one of them proud." His voice cracked. "It was supposed to be harmless. But it was a mistake —one stupid, awful mistake."

The words emptied him; his posture caved as the last of that polished helpfulness slid away.

Somewhere down the road, a siren began to rise—steady, purposeful, closing the distance.

Beside me, Callie exhaled softly. Her camera hung unused from its strap. She'd taken a few stills earlier, nothing more— just documentation, no exploitation.

Jason's RCMP truck rolled into the lot, lights flashing muted colours against the silver car. Charlie didn't run. He just sat there on the bumper, shoulders caved in, staring at his hands.

The cruiser stopped. Jason stepped out, boots crunching on gravel. He approached with that measured calm he always brought to scenes like this.

"Charlie Campbell. I need you to come with me."

Charlie stood slowly, mechanically. "I can still call a lawyer, right?"

"You should."

As they walked toward the cruiser, Charlotte stood frozen beside the car, one hand over her mouth—not crying, just absorbing the weight of what her careless words and Charlie's desperate loyalty had wrought.

I stepped back as the cruiser doors closed, as everything that had been building all week finally resolved into something simple and terrible.

Callie lowered her camera completely. "Is it over?"

"For Charlie, yeah." I watched the cruiser pull away, lights still flashing. "For the rest of us... we'll see."

The wind shifted, carrying the last traces of festival music from the square. Volunteers continued their wrap-up, oblivious to what had just unfolded. By noon, the Aurora Nights Festival would be officially over—ending not with applause, but quiet cleanup.

But some things had shifted in ways that wouldn't reset so easily.

Des pressed against my leg. Charlotte finally moved, getting into her car without a word. The silver sedan pulled away slowly, heading not toward the airport but back into town.

"She didn't know," Callie said quietly. "Did she?"

I thought about Charlotte's genuine confusion when Charlie claimed she'd authorized the reserved box—the shock on her face when he confessed. "No. She was just... careless. Vain. Said things without thinking about how they'd be heard."

"And he heard them as orders."

"He heard what he wanted to hear. Permission to prove himself indispensable."

The parking lot felt larger now, emptier. Morning sun caught on broken glass near the dumpster, making it sparkle.

"Come on. Let's see this through."

We walked back toward the main square, where the festival's final hour was already ticking down. The truth had made less noise than I'd expected—a quiet confession in a parking lot, witnessed by three people and a dog.

But it had been loud enough.

By the time we reached the main square, the morning had that hollow feel of a crisis slowly unwinding. Vendor stalls stood half-collapsed, volunteers moving with the tired efficiency of people who just wanted to be done and go home. The festival wasn't officially over yet—that would come at noon—but already people were packing up, cutting their losses and heading home early.

Des trotted ahead, nose working the ground where a cotton-candy cart had been earlier. Callie walked beside me, her camera bouncing at her hip.

We found Jason near the bandstand, talking with two plain-clothes officers I recognized from Major Crimes. He glanced up as we approached, gave a small nod, then finished speaking before stepping away.

"It's official. Charlie's been charged—manslaughter and obstruction. He's cooperating."

"And Dawn's death?"

"Closed. Accidental death from toxic inhalation." Jason's jaw tightened. "He'll do time, but not what he would've if it had been premeditated."

Callie shifted her weight. "What about the memorial box theft?"

Jason glanced around, then dropped his voice. "Charlie admitted to taking it on someone else's orders. Wouldn't say who, but we know who gives orders in this town. That's a separate investigation now—one the Bugles won't shake off easily."

"Good," I said, though it didn't feel like victory.

A small crowd had gathered near the bandstand—reporters with cameras and recording equipment, a few locals who'd heard something was happening. Word had spread that the festival committee was holding a brief press conference to address the arrest.

Charlotte stood off to one side, talking quietly with someone who might have been her lawyer or just moral support. Her usual polished confidence had thinned to something brittle, careful.

A television crew from Winnipeg was setting up—the same one that had been covering the festival since Friday. A radio reporter tested her microphone. The local paper's photographer adjusted his lens.

"She's really doing this," Callie said.

"Looks that way."

When the cameras turned on, Charlotte stepped forward. No podium, no prepared notes—just Charlotte in her festival jacket, looking tired under the late-morning sun.

"I want to address what happened this morning," she began, her voice steady but lacking its usual brightness. "Charlie Campbell has been charged in connection with Dawn Kessler's death. The RCMP has classified it as accidental toxic inhalation caused by tampering with an Aurora Fire packet."

A reporter called out a question, but Charlotte shook her head.

"Let me finish. Charlie worked closely with me throughout the festival planning. I trusted him. I defended him. And I failed to see what he was doing." Her voice caught slightly, then steadied. "That's on me—not the festival committee, not the volunteers, not this community. Me."

Another pause. The wind picked up, rattling the microphones.

"Dawn Kessler came to Balsam Bay to document something beautiful. She deserved better than what happened to her. Her family deserves better. This community deserves better." Charlotte's hands clenched at her sides. "I'll be making a formal statement at the closing ceremony at noon, but I wanted to speak directly to the media first. No spin. No excuses. Just the truth."

The reporters erupted with questions, but Charlotte was already walking away, her lawyer moving to intercept the press while she disappeared into the crowd.

"Wow," Callie breathed after a long beat. "She actually meant that."

"Pride only carries you so far," I said. "Eventually you run out of places to hide."

Jason's radio crackled, the sound oddly loud against the hush settling over the square. He listened for a moment, then nodded to us. "Major Crimes is wrapping up at the campground. Scene's cleared and officially released."

Around us, the square continued its slow transformation from festival space back to normal town centre. The vendors who'd stayed were packing up now—boxes of unsold merchandise, folded tarps, empty propane tanks waiting to be collected. A few families still wandered between the remaining booths, determined to squeeze out the last moments of their weekend adventure.

Near the craft tent, I spotted Mandy distributing leftover pastries to volunteers. She waved when she saw us, then went back to making sure everyone got fed before cleanup finished.

Across the square, Fern stood in the middle of a group of volunteers, clipboard in hand, directing traffic with surprising authority.

"Marco, those chairs go to the community centre. Linda, can you check the first-aid stations one more time? We need to make sure nothing's left behind." Her voice carried clearly, no hesitation, no apology in her posture. "Good. Now let's break down the tables before the ceremony starts."

The volunteers moved without question. Fern made a note on her clipboard and moved on to the next crisis, coordinating the breakdown with the same confidence she'd brought to her astronomy sessions all week.

"She's different," Callie observed.

"She's the same," I said. "Just finally letting everyone else see it."

A burst of laughter carried from where a group of volunteers were wrestling with a stubborn tent pole. Fern walked over, assessed the situation, and gave quick, clear instructions. The tent pole came free to a round of cheers. Fern grinned, jotted another note, and moved on without breaking stride.

Near the refreshment table, I noticed Arlo hovering at the edge of things—not quite part of the volunteer efforts, but not absent either. When Fern glanced his way, he gave a small nod. She returned it and kept working.

Something in their body language spoke of understanding reached, bridges slowly being rebuilt. Not fixed—not yet, but maybe on their way.

Jason checked his watch. "Closing ceremony starts soon. You staying?"

"Wouldn't miss it."

The square was nearly empty now, wind tugging at the last of the bunting. Volunteers moved like ghosts between the tents, packing away the week.

Jason let out a slow breath. "Good." He managed a weary smile. "You saw it before any of us."

"Just following patterns."

"Maybe next time I'll listen sooner."

The words hung between us—not quite an apology, but close enough.

People were starting to drift toward the bandstand area, finding spots to stand or sit for the official ceremony. Some unfolded chairs they'd retrieved from their cars. Others claimed small patches of grass. The crowd was smaller than it had been during the festival's peak, but still substantial—maybe a hundred people, volunteers and visitors mixed together, locals who wanted to see how the town would close out a week that had been both triumphant and tragic.

The sun had climbed higher, warming the air enough that jackets came off and thermoses got refilled one last time. The October light had that particular quality—gold edging toward amber, the sun already lower than it had been yesterday.

"Mom." Callie had stopped walking, her phone in her hand. "I want to show you something before I post it."

She turned the screen toward me. The post was ready, hovering on the publish screen:

The Aurora Nights Festival ends today, at noon.

Over the past week, this community came together to celebrate something beautiful—the northern lights, the landscape we call home, the connections that make small towns work.

But we also witnessed something harder: the cost of silence, the weight of expectations, the damage that happens when loyalty becomes harmful.

Dawn Kessler died here. That's a fact. Charlie Campbell has been charged in connection with her death. That's also a fact.

What happens next is up to all of us—how we tell this story, what lessons we take from it, whether we choose truth over comfort.

Sometimes light shows beauty. Sometimes it shows what we'd rather not see.

Either way, it's still light.

Thank you to everyone who made this festival possible. Thank you to the volunteers, the visitors, the community members who showed up even when things got complicated.

We'll see you next year. Under new management, with old values.

Below the text sat a single photo—the northern lights over Aurora Point, taken Thursday night before everything fell apart. Green and violet curtains dancing against the dark, reflected in the lake below. Beautiful and untouched by human complications.

She hesitated, thumb hovering above the screen.

"Post it," I said.

The post went live, a tiny circle spinning like a held breath.

"There," she said quietly. "That's the truth. Not all of it, but enough."

"More than enough," I said.

The crowd around the bandstand was filling in now. Mabel had appeared with her clipboard, organizing things with the same efficient authority she'd brought to every festival meeting. Volunteers adjusted microphones and tested sound levels.

"Come on," I said to Callie and Des. "Let's find a spot before it gets too crowded."

We found a place near the edge, close enough to hear but with room for Des to settle without being in anyone's way. The dog stretched out at my feet with a contented sigh, finally able to rest after days of festival excitement.

Jason appeared beside us, handing Callie a cup of cocoa he'd grabbed from the refreshment table.

"Think the truce lasts till Tuesday?" he asked, nodding

toward where CLAIM and LANTERN volunteers were working side by side.

"Maybe Wednesday." She smiled faintly.

"Optimist," he said, though his mouth quirked.

The square had that particular feeling of an ending—not quite sadness, not quite relief, but something in between. The knowledge that something significant had happened here, and now it was time to acknowledge it properly and move forward.

The Aurora Nights Festival was coming to its end—banners packed, its lights dimmed.

But first, the town needed to say goodbye properly.

CHAPTER TWENTY

By noon, the square had filled for one final gathering. The exhaustion that had ruled all week seemed to lift slightly, replaced by something that felt like cautious relief.

Des had found a patch of sun near the bandstand and stretched out in lazy contentment. Her tail thumped now and then when someone stopped to scratch her ears—the festival's official mascot, still working the crowd like a pro.

Callie stood beside me, camera hanging idle around her neck. She'd taken enough photos this week. Sometimes you just needed to be present without documenting every moment.

The noon bells from Balsam Bay United rang out—clear, simple, final. People turned toward the bandstand where Mayor John Bugle stepped to the microphone. Pressed shirt, festival jacket—formal armour over strain. His knuckles whitened as he gripped the podium.

"Thank you to everyone who made this year's Aurora Nights possible," he began, his voice carrying practiced confidence. "We come together each fall to celebrate light—this year we've been reminded how precious that light is."

He paused.

"Our community grieves the loss of visitor Dawn Kessler. Charges have been laid against Charlie Campbell in connection with her death. Justice will take its course. On behalf of the council, I offer condolences to her family and gratitude to all who supported the investigation."

The words came out clean, rehearsed. But they landed like stones on still water—brief ripples, no depth. The applause was polite and died quickly.

Beside me, Des shifted her weight, ears forward.

Charlotte stepped up next, fingers woven tight, shoulders drawn. When she spoke, her voice was quieter than I'd ever heard it. For the first time all week, she wasn't performing.

"No festival is worth a life. We owe each other better."

A few people shifted. Someone coughed.

"I failed to see what was happening right in front of me." Her voice wavered, then steadied. "I can't undo it, but I can own it. I'm stepping down from the festival committee, effective today."

The crowd's reaction was muted—no cheers, just a low murmur. A few people nodded. Others looked away. Charlotte stood there a moment longer, then stepped back with that same fragile composure.

Mabel moved to the microphone, clipboard under her arm, her voice warm with practiced authority. "Representing the Balsam Bay Heritage Museum and the astronomy club, please welcome Fern Carrick."

Fern walked to the mic with steadiness I hadn't seen in her before. No clipboard, no nervous adjustments. Just a single folded page in her hand and calm that seemed to rise from somewhere steadier than the week's chaos.

She looked out over the square, took a breath, and began.

"This week tested all of us. But it also showed what holds firm—our curiosity, our patience, our care for this place."

Her voice didn't shake. Didn't rush.

"Whether you came for the science or the spectacle, the aurora belongs to everyone. We understand it best when we stand under it together."

Real applause followed this time. Not polite—genuine. Even John Bugle clapped, though his expression stayed carefully neutral.

Callie leaned closer. "She's really come into her own."

"Maybe the town finally noticed."

The band struck up a slow, familiar tune. Volunteers moved through the crowd with thermoses of cocoa. I watched a CLAIM equipment manager pour a cup for a LANTERN coordinator, both laughing when some sloshed over the rim.

It reminded me of a search winding down—that quiet moment when everyone knows the missing piece is found, even if what's left behind isn't whole. Relief doesn't come as celebration. It comes as release.

Charlotte stood near the edge of the crowd, head bowed while an older woman spoke quietly to her. She listened, nodded, then looked toward Fern and applauded once—soft, deliberate, as if conceding something she hadn't been ready to give up.

The music filled the square again. Adults swayed with paper cups warming their hands. A few teenagers threw a frisbee near the information booth. The afternoon light carried that soft October warmth, gentle but already fading.

Des pressed against my leg. I scratched behind her ears and watched the square resettle into something that looked almost normal.

Callie was scrolling through her phone, her expression

shifting to something like satisfaction. "Comments are kind today. People saying they're glad the truth came out. That the town handled it with grace."

"Did we?"

She looked up. "We're trying to. That counts for something."

A gust of wind scattered paper napkins across the grass. Volunteers chased them down, calling to each other as they caught them. The band played on, notes drifting over the square like leaves falling in no particular hurry.

Charlotte moved through the dispersing crowd alone, her posture still straight but her steps slower. A few people nodded as she passed. Most didn't. She accepted both with the same quiet dignity.

"She'll be okay," Callie said, watching her go.

"Eventually."

Fern stood near the refreshment table now, surrounded by a small group asking questions about next year's programming. She answered each one with patience, her earlier nervousness replaced by a quiet confidence. Arlo hovered at the edge of the group, not quite part of the conversation but close enough to signal support. When Fern glanced his way, he gave a small nod. She returned it and kept talking.

Within the hour, the square was already emptying. Families folded blankets, vendors stacked boxes, and the band closed with one last, unhurried tune before packing their gear.

Jason checked his watch. "I should get back to the detachment. Paperwork won't file itself."

"Never does."

He hesitated. "You did good work this week, Til. Don't let anyone tell you otherwise."

"Not planning to."

His mouth quirked. "Didn't think you were."

After he left, Callie and I helped stack chairs and collect stray cups. The work was simple, rhythmic.

By the time we finished, the sun had dropped low enough to paint the lake in copper and rose. The square settled into what looked like any other Sunday evening in Balsam Bay.

Except it wasn't. Not quite.

The festival was over, but the weight of what had happened during it still pressed against the edges of everything. Dawn Kessler's name would be remembered here long after the bunting faded. Charlie Campbell's choices would ripple through this community for years.

But today, at least, the town had come together under string lights and tried to remember why it mattered.

Callie tucked her phone into her pocket. "Ready to go home?"

"Almost."

I lingered a moment longer, watching the last volunteers carry boxes toward the community centre. The breeze off the lake was cool enough to sting, carrying the clean bite of water edged with cedar. Somewhere down the hill, someone laughed —quick, relieved, the sound of normal life resuming.

I turned toward the truck and stopped. Three familiar faces stood in a neat row, each wearing the same mix of pride and triumph.

"Well," Enid said as I approached, "we provided quite the civic contribution, didn't we?"

Nora clasped her hands in front of her chest. "Imagine it —after all these years of keeping this town running on gossip alone, we finally have something useful to brag about."

Trish gave a dignified nod. "Public service takes many forms. Ours just happens to include a bit of eavesdropping and excellent intuition."

"You three did more than eavesdrop," I said. "You found the missing link that solved the case."

"Oh, we know," Enid said, beaming. "But thank you for saying it out loud where witnesses can hear."

Nora sniffed, half-mock offended. "Some of us were beginning to think no one appreciated our vigilance."

Trish smiled, satisfied. "I'd say we've earned a mention in the next town newsletter. Perhaps a commendation from the mayor—once he's done apologizing for his family."

I laughed. "I'll see what I can do."

Enid patted my arm. "That's all we ask, dear. Just proper credit and maybe front-row seats at the next scandal."

They linked arms and set off toward the café, already debating which headline would sound best. Their voices drifted after them—bright, familiar, and unreasonably proud —and for once, I couldn't blame them.

Des sat beside my boot, patient as always.

"All right, girl. Let's go."

We walked back toward the truck with Callie as the first stars began to appear overhead. The aurora wouldn't return tonight—the forecast had been clear about that. But somehow the sky felt fuller anyway.

The Belles' laughter carried down the street long after they turned the corner, softening the edges of the day. I stood there a moment, watching sunlight catch on the lake beyond the trees. Balsam Bay felt steady again—held together by gossip, goodwill, and a few women who never stopped paying attention.

Later that evening, supper dishes sat stacked beside the sink, the smell of roast chicken and mashed potatoes still lingering in the air. The wood stove ticked softly, throwing steady warmth across the small kitchen. Des snored in her spot near the hearth, one paw twitching as if she were chasing some harmless dream.

Callie sat at the table with her laptop open, a half-finished mug of cocoa beside her. The screen's glow caught in her hair as she scrolled, pausing to edit a line, then smiling faintly.

I poured two mugs of coffee as boots sounded on the back steps. Jason knocked once out of habit before letting himself in.

"Coffee?"

He gave a grateful nod, taking a seat. "Feels strange, doesn't it? One minute the whole town's upside down, next minute it's Sunday night again."

"That's Balsam Bay. We go from chaos to calm faster than the weather forecast changes."

Jason pulled out a chair and sat down. "Got some news for you, Callie. Digital forensics traced the suspicious accounts behind those comments on your blog. All of them were created under a single IP—Charlie Campbell's home router."

Callie blinked. "You're kidding."

He shook his head. "Nope. We don't know if he acted on his own or if he was… encouraged, but we're looking into it."

Callie let out a slow breath. "Well, that explains a few things. My account's back, by the way—turns out someone reported me for 'spreading misinformation,' which I'm guessing was Charlie, too. It triggered an automated suspension until they reviewed it." She gave a dry little laugh. "Guess I passed the algorithm's moral exam."

Jason smiled faintly. "Glad to hear it. The town could use your voice right now."

Callie hit a key on her laptop with a flourish. "Speaking of which—final post's up. People are being kind for once. Someone commented, *Aurora Nights ends, but the light lingers.*"

"That's good," Jason said. "True, too."

Her mouth curved. "I tried to keep it honest."

"You did," I said. "Your grandfather would've been proud of that."

Jason leaned back, mug cradled in both hands again. "We're ready to release the memorial box. If you want to come by tomorrow and sign the release, I'll have the paperwork ready. Charlie admitted he passed the contents along before dumping it behind the community centre."

Jason didn't need to say who. We both knew.

I felt that familiar tightening in my chest. "Then they've got whatever was in there."

"Looks that way."

Callie closed her laptop with a soft click. "So the question is —what were they looking for?"

"Dad's research," Jason said. "Whatever he'd been working on about the mine, the town's history, mineral rights."

"Or," I said slowly, "it's a message."

The silence that followed was heavier than anything we'd said aloud.

Jason set his mug down carefully. "You think they're telling us they know."

"Think about it. We staged a whole memorial service. Had half the town there. Everything looked right, felt right—the grief was real enough even if the death wasn't." I traced the rim of my mug. "And then someone disrupts it at exactly the right moment, steals the box, and now the Bugles have whatever Bertha packed inside."

"They already know Dad's alive," Callie said quietly. "Gus confessed to staging the canoe accident. So why steal from the memorial?"

"Because they want us to know that they're onto us," Jason said.

The circular logic made my head hurt, but it was the only explanation that fit.

"It's a power play," I continued. "They can't expose Dad without admitting what they did—why he had to disappear in the first place. But they can take his things right in front of us and make sure we understand the message."

"That we're not fooling anyone," Callie finished.

Jason leaned back, the chair creaking. "So the memorial didn't work. They saw right through it."

"Or they're just reminding us they're watching. That they can reach us whenever they want."

Des shifted on the rug, her tail thumping once. Outside, wind tapped against the kitchen window.

"What worries me more," Jason said, "is what was actually in that box. Bertha packed it—photos, Dad's reading glasses, some personal effects. But she also mentioned papers from his desk."

I nodded. "His research."

"Maybe. Or just random documents—letters, receipts, old notes. We don't know what she grabbed."

"But the Bugles have it now," Callie said.

"Could be nothing," I said, though I didn't believe it. "Could be everything."

"Could be whatever Dad discovered that made him dangerous enough to want him gone," Jason said quietly.

The thought sat heavy between us.

"He left us that message. Told us he was alive, that we were in danger. But he didn't tell us what he'd found."

"Probably safer that way," Jason said. "The less we know, the less we can accidentally reveal."

I looked at both of them across the table—my brother and my daughter, the only two people in the world who shared this impossible burden.

"We're still standing. The Bugles made a move and we didn't break. We kept the performance going even when it got hard."

Jason nodded slowly. "Looks that way." He drained his coffee and stood, shrugging on his jacket. "Get some rest, okay?"

"You too."

He squeezed my shoulder as he passed. At the door he paused, pulling a folded newspaper from his jacket pocket. "Almost forgot—wanted you to see this."

He tossed it on the table. The Balsam Bay Gazette, today's edition. A small article in the lower corner of the front page, easy to miss if you weren't looking.

Numbered Company Completes Ridge Purchase

Local speculation continues about buyer's identity and development plans

"That numbered company finally closed the deal on the ridge property," Jason said. "They've been cutting access roads up there for months. Now they own the place outright—land, timber, and whatever's buried underneath."

I glanced at the article. The property description was vague, but the implications were clear. Someone had just acquired a significant piece of land outside Balsam Bay, and nobody knew who or why.

"Funny how these things work," Jason continued. "A mining outfit was trying to stake a claim on that same land. But when the sale went through, their paperwork died on the vine."

"That can't have gone over well."

"No," he said. "And I'm sure it won't end there." He pulled open the door, letting in a gust of cold air. "Anyway, town's buzzing the new owner. Some people think it's just another logging outfit. Others are convinced it's something bigger." He shrugged. "Guess we'll find out eventually."

The door shut, and Des lifted her head, listening until the footsteps faded.

Callie reached for the paper, scanning the article. "A numbered company. That's a pretty standard way to hide who's really behind a purchase."

"Very standard." I stared at the newsprint, that familiar unease settling in my chest. "Question is, why hide it?"

"Maybe they knew people would object if they knew who was buying."

"Or maybe they didn't want certain other buyers to know they were interested." I thought about the Bugles, about their grip on this town, about how mineral rights kept surfacing in conversations I didn't fully understand yet. "Jason said a mining outfit lost their claim to that land."

We sat in silence for a moment, the only sound the wood stove ticking and Des's gentle snoring.

"Do you think it's connected?" Callie asked finally. "To Grandpa's research? To whatever the Bugles are so worried about?"

"I don't know." I folded the paper and set it aside. "But I don't like how many paths in this town keep leading back to mineral rights and land deals."

Callie stretched, setting her laptop aside. "I'm heading up. Need something that doesn't involve conspiracies for a while."

"Hot chocolate still counts as self-care."

She smiled. "Maybe I'll make some."

As she moved toward the kitchen, I glanced out the living room window. Beyond the birches, the dark outline of the store sat quiet, its windows catching a faint reflection of the northern sky. And somewhere beyond that, in the darkness, the ridge property sat waiting—newly purchased by someone who didn't want their name attached to the deal.

Des stirred and padded to my side, tail sweeping the floor. Outside, a thin green ribbon of light arched low across the horizon—subtle, steady, beautiful. The kind of aurora only locals bothered to notice.

"I wonder where you are tonight, Dad. I hope you're seeing this too."

Des leaned her head against my leg, a warm, wordless answer.

"Mom, cocoa's ready."

I smiled, turning from the window. "On my way."

Des bounded ahead, claws clicking softly on the wood floor. I followed, the scent of chocolate drifting to meet me.

The aurora shimmered once more, faint but certain, and outside the wind had calmed; even the birches stood still. The town was quiet again—and for the first time all week, at peace.

You've reached the end of *Death at Aurora Point.*
Some mysteries are solved—others are coming to light.
Tilly has seen how far some will go to protect their secrets...
and how much she stands to lose if she lets them win.
But Balsam Bay has never been one for quiet winters.
And when new footprints appear on the frozen ridge, another
mystery begins.

Continue the story now in
Death at Diamond Hill
Book Three in the Tilly Lafleur Mystery series.

Visit MaisieGraves.com for details.

STAY IN THE LOOP

Want more Balsam Bay?

Join my newsletter for new book updates, behind-the-scenes notes, and the occasional appearance from Des.

New subscribers also receive a free short mystery set in Balsam Bay.

Sign up at: MaisieGraves.com/newsletter.

No spam. No noise. Just thoughtful mysteries and good company.

THANKS FOR READING

Thank you for spending time with Tilly, Callie, and Des in Balsam Bay.

If you enjoyed the story, I'd be grateful if you left a review. Even a few words make a difference and help other readers find the series.

There's more to uncover in Balsam Bay—and the story isn't over yet.

ALSO BY MAISIE GRAVES

Tilly Lafleur Mysteries

Death at Balsam Bay

Death at Aurora Point

Death at Diamond Hill

Death at Melvin House

Short Stories from Balsam Bay

Whispers in the Snow

The Disappearing Scarecrow

Snow on the Airwaves

Discover all of Maisie's books and formats at

MaisieGraves.com/books

ABOUT THE AUTHOR

Maisie Graves writes small-town cozy mysteries with real stakes and buried secrets.

Her Tilly Lafleur series follows an amateur sleuth as each case pulls her deeper into a town she thought she knew.

Maisie lives in Canada and is always working on the next mystery.

maisiegraves.com

facebook.com/maisiegravesauthor

instagram.com/maisiegravesauthor

goodreads.com/maisiegravesauthor

bookbub.com/authors/maisie-graves